MW01206567

To my family for which this would have never been finished.

Every day you make me a better writer and a better person.

You are forever my inspiration.

Table of Contents

Chapter One

The sun blazed in through the treetops lighting up the forest floor. The underbrush rustled with life. A bird called out in the distance. She felt her heartbeat in tune with the noises of the trees as she traveled through them. She was in her woods. As she walked deeper into the forest, a light fog settled on the ground and a soft breeze rustled through the trees, blowing the fallen leaves towards her. Her hair flowed behind her with the wind as she followed a buck, clenching her bow tighter as she hopped over a fallen branch. In her mind's eye, she could sense the buck's heart racing and his lungs heaving with air. Ailia felt him begin to pant as she saw him slow. The trees thinned out to reveal a small meadow with a trickling stream running through it. She stopped at the edge of the forest, catching sight of the buck drinking from the water. She found a tree with a low hanging branch and jumped, grabbing the branch to hoist herself up. With the buck in her sights, she readied her bow and pulled it back. After a deep breath, she let the arrow fly with a soft twang.

Ailia blinked, fully awake, and groaned sitting straight up for an instant. She fell back on the bed.

She shivered slightly but then sighed and chalked it up to an overactive imagination as she got out of bed.

After putting on a pair of her leather work pants and a sleeveless shirt, she walked out to the kitchen, braiding her long, dark red hair as she went. She found her father starting the fire and her mother attempting to knead bread. Ailia glanced at her mother and noticed her graying hair remained uncombed and her dress was the same one she had been wearing for the last week. She shook her head as she walked over by the front door.

"Good morninnnng, Ailia," her mom said hiccupping as she tried to move the dough around the wooden counter.

"Morning Mamm," Ailia replied, putting on her apron and grabbing a basket lined with a soft blanket.

As Ailia started to walk out the door, her mother made a small grunt. Ailia turned and saw that the dough had stuck to the counter and Rhona's hands. She gave one more feeble attempt to knead it and then gave up. She left the countertop and walked away bobbling slightly. She sat at the table and took a long drink out of a bottle.

"Could you...," She asked, trailing off as she took another drink.

Ailia nodded as she set her basket down and went over to the counter. She quickly kneaded the bread dough and placed it by the fire to rise. Her mother hiccuped again and laid her head on the table. Ailia shook her head and grabbed her basket before slowly walking out to the small wooden hen house next to the barn on the right side of the house. The chickens were clucking, and from the barn, she could hear the soft neighing of horses. She climbed the ramp up to the door and freed the chickens. They scampered past Ailia, and she ducked inside, letting the screen door bang shut behind her.

"I'll need to muck this out tonight," she muttered to herself while picking a dozen and half fresh brown eggs from the nests and tucked them in her basket before hurrying back into the fresh air. She smiled and placed the basket of eggs down near the front door of the feed shed. Inside Ailia grabbed a small bucket of table scraps from last night's dinner.

She walked slowly, throwing the slop around, and the chickens quickly gathered around their breakfast. Ailia headed to the back to the feed shed for the rest of the table scraps from last night's dinner to add to the pig trough along with a few bunches of turnips. As she neared the pen, the pigs ran up to the trough and happily chomped at the food as Ailia poured it in.

Ailia looked in at the little piglets and was happy to see that they were all doing well and fattening up nicely. She took the empty feed bucket and headed to grab the eggs she had left near the feed shed before heading back into the house.

Waylin, her father, shuffled in behind her with a block of wood and a small knife in his gnarled hands. He kicked off his boots and sat at the table.

"How do you want your eggs this morning, Pap?" she smiled and held up one of the eggs.

"Same as always, I don't know why you bother asking," Waylin mumbled, "insolent child" as he fiddled with his block and started to carve out chunks of wood.

Ailia pretended not to hear the rest of her father's half uttered insults and instead focused on her mother, "And you, Mamm?"

Rhona, her mother, hiccupped and took a long drink from her bottle. She mumbled "Scrammmmbled."

Ailia grabbed six eggs from the day before and put the fresh eggs from her basket into the lined crate for market. Ailia moved to the fire and took the small cast iron pan off its hook. With the tongs, she quickly made an indention in the coals for the pan. She cracked two eggs for her father, humming a light melody as the whites bubbled.

"Would you quit with that awful noise."

Ailia froze and stopped humming, concentrating on the eggs.

"How's the farm? You're not slacking off are you," Waylin asked, not looking up from his task.

"It's doing really good," Ailia answered quickly, "I'm going to harvest what I can today and take the extra eggs to the market and then pick up supplies for canning," She paused as she put his eggs on a plate and handed them to him with an excited smile before continuing, "And then I think I'm going hunting in a few days."

Waylin grabbed the plate with one hand and her wrist with the other and his dark eyes looked into hers, "You will do no such thing unless I say you can. You're not to go out in those woods alone, you hear me. A stupid girl like you is likely to get lost."

Ailia bit her tongue and lowered her gaze nodding her head. Waylin squeezed her wrist until she wanted to cry out. She didn't make a sound, but a single tear rolled down her cheek before he released his grip. Ailia quickly went back to the pan and made the rest of the eggs before moving the pan to the edge of the fire to cool.

"Doooo ya havvve any anything else planned?" her mom asked, as she grabbed her plate from Ailia and nearly dumped the whole thing on the table as she set it down in front of her.

"Well, like I said I'm going to head to the market and then after I plan on making a few preparations for canning," she paused and hastily added, "if that's alright that is."

"Would you pick up some flour and spirits for me?" Rhona asked as she picked up some of her eggs. She fumbled with her fork and the eggs fell all over the plate and table.

Ailia tried not to roll her eyes at the mess she would now have to clean up. She sighed but replied, "Sure, won't be a problem, Ma."

"Well, go if you must, but don't be too long." Waylin rasped, his voice scratching Ailia's ears like porcupine needles. He coughed slightly and cleared his throat, "Wouldn't want anything to be neglected. Remember last time."

Ailia flinched and rubbed her cheek, nodding hastily. She finished eating her eggs in hasty silence, eager to get the meal over with. When everyone was finished, she boiled some water and quickly washed the breakfast dishes, put them away and then cleaned the table of wood scraps and cold scrambled eggs.

She pushed the bread from the edge of the fire into the coals before grabbing her basket from beside the door and pulling her clippers off their hook on the wall. She headed outside into the bright morning, humming a soft melody now that she was out of her father's earshot.

"Good morning, my plants," she sang as her farm plot came into view. "What do you have for me this morning?" Ailia looked and swore she could see her plants jump to attention. Her skin prickled, her vision becoming hazy for a moment as their leaves unfurled to the sun. She thought she could even see new produce grow right before her eyes. She swore that the beans shot out from their stalks and yellow tomatoes turned red before her. The sight stopped her in her tracks and she blinked a few times. A chicken clucked and pecked at her already scuffed work boot. She dragged her eyes down and gently waved the chicken away. When she looked at her plants again, they were back to their normal vibrant green selves.

She shook it off as she walked up to her wagon. She checked over the empty bushels in the back and noticed several small holes in a few of them. Sighing, she went to the supply room in the barn and grabbed a few straw bands and her needle and twine. She went back to the wagon and made quick work of pulling out the damaged bands. With nimble fingers, Ailia wove the new bands into place and whipped stitched them to the surrounding bands of the bushel for added stability. She stashed the extra straw and twine into the seat of the wagon and got to harvesting.

Ailia checked the corn first, but it was still too early for the ears. Instead, she pulled weeds as she went, plucking out the rare tall encroaching grass that liked to twine itself around the stalks of corn, temporarily stashing them in her apron. The next rows were tomatoes. She worked quickly clipping the bright red ones off their vines in groups of three or four. At the end of only the second row, Ailia looked down and realized her first bushel was already full. She took a second look and realized the tomatoes she had harvested were much bigger than any of the ones she had ever grown before.

A strange tingle formed on her skin as if the answers to her questions lay on the tip of her tongue. Only she dare not speak or even think of what this might be.

Ailia sighed, trying to shake off the feeling and carried the full bushel to the wagon and secured it before heading back to the house. She pulled the bread from the fire and set it to cool. As she turned to go back out to the farm she noticed that Rhona had left an empty bottle overturned on the table. Ailia put the bottle down in the cellar and went back out to the field. She finished harvesting the tomatoes, filling most of one of the large crates. For the rows of root vegetables, she thinned the greens by pulling out the larger ones and leaving the younger ones to grow longer.

she thought as she piled the harvested roots near the wagon as she went. When she had finished with all the rows of beets, potatoes, carrots, and turnips, she shook most of the extra dirt off of them and sorted them into their respective bushels. The extra roots were put into crates and, combined, filled nearly three of them. Ailia moved the full crates up to the side of the house and grabbed one of the remaining empty bushels and moved on to her green beans and spring peas.

She continued on as the sun rose higher in the sky to meet the midpoint. Much to Ailia's surprise she did, in fact, fill a bushel of both green beans and spring peas as well as a full crate of the two mixed together. She secured the bushels in the back of the wagon and took stock of the harvest so far. A wide grin spread across her face.

Ailia looked up at the sun and gauged the distance to midpoint before muttering to herself, "Focus, Ailia. I should have just enough time to harvest the berries before I have to make lunch."

She moved to her berry bushes and picked blackberries, purple berries and red berries, thinning out the bushes with her shears as she went. Just like the vegetables, the fruit also seemed much larger. Ailla took one of the purple berries and weighed it in her hand before biting into it. Juice ran down her chin as the sweet flesh exploded on her taste buds.

and so sweet. She finished the berry and wiped the remaining juice off her chin before filling the last open bushel for the market with a mixture of berries, and she still had enough to fill at least two more bushels. As Ailia picked her last red berry, Rhona stumbled out of the house to see what was keeping her.

"Ailiaaaaa," she called.

Ailia stood from her plants and carried her last basket to the wagon.

"Oh, there you are," Rhona giggled.

"Yes, Mamm?"

"What's taking so long? We're starvvvvving! You're slacking child," Rhona shouted as she leaned against the house.

"I'm sorry. I'll be right in to make lunch, Mamm. Why don't you go in and sit down."

Rhona nodded and went back into the house, stumbling and falling down once along the way. Ailia shook her head and wiped her brow with the back of her hand as she walked over to grab a large crate for the extra berries. She carefully dumped the berries into the crate and set it near the front porch. She walked back to her plants and cleaned up, throwing the trimmings and weeds into the compost. Ailia went to the porch and started to move the crates into the cellar.

"Mamm?" she asked, after she had put all the crates in the cellar and grabbed out her family's share to fill the hanging baskets near the window.

"Yes?"

"Do you think a person could talk to plants or sense animals?" Ailia asked as she sliced one of the fresh loaves of bread for sandwiches. "Maybe even have them respond? I mean kinda like Magick. I always like to think that's how the mages do it, you know, they sort of communicate with their element."

Rhona turned to her daughter and with a roll of her eyes replied, "That's pure foolishness, and you know very well that they can't. Magick is just a hoax. Any person who claims to be able to do it is just trying to weave a tale. You never see Magick in public because it doesn't exist."

Ailia sighed and went back down into the cellar and grabbed a chunk of cured meat.

Ailia thought as she climbed back up to the kitchen with deliberate steps. She put the chunk of meat down on the counter and looked out the window. Her skin prickled again as a few angry clouds rolled in. They looked as angry as she felt. Grabbing a cluster of tomatoes from the basket, she began to slice them up. She layered the ingredients on the bread. As she worked, her Mamm rang the lunch bell and her Pa emerged from the workshop attached to the barn carrying the same chunk of wood from breakfast. He sat at the table and, as she set his plate in front of him, she almost asked her father about what she and her mother had discussed, but she knew his answer would be the same and his tongue lashing worse. The clouds above them rumbled. She hated that they were so closed minded.

They ate in silence and, when everyone was done, she cleaned the scraps into a bucket for the pigs before washing up the dishes. She put the dishes away and then went to her room. She untied the money pouch from her belt and changed into a simple blue full length dress with a dusty trim that used to be white. She pulled on a long sweater to cover the red mark left by Waylin earlier in the day. Ailia slipped the money pouch into a hidden pocket of the dress.

Ailia shuddered at the thought as she finished getting ready by tying a ribbon into her braid. As she shut her bedroom door she thought, *Perhaps Kiana will have some advice for me.*

Ailia sighed and went out to the barn. She bridled her deep brown horse, Solas, and hitched her up to the wagon before heading into town.

Chapter Two

Latzu was about five miles southwest of their home. Ailia knew the dirt path well. As she traveled under a low hanging section of trees, a squirrel jumped down from a branch and landed on her shoulder. She turned and looked at him with a soft smile as she petted him.

"Hello, McLeod," she whispered as she offered him a nut from her sweater pocket. McLeod gratefully took the nut and gnawed on it as Ailia drove through the quiet woods. As she got closer to town, McLeod pawed at her face and then jumped up into the last tree she passed before the road widened and houses started to appear. Ailia steered her horse down the main road past weathered buildings and headed straight to the market store. She hitched her horse and wagon to the post pausing to pet the ivory star on Solas's nose, before heading inside. As the door closed behind her, Ailia greeted the girl behind the counter.

"What do you have for us today?" Prudence asked Ailia.

"Well, quite a bit actually. All fresh, today, I'm afraid. I didn't have time to get in the kitchen. I'm planning on canning later this week, but I'm going to need some more supplies."

"Let's see," Prudence said, as she walked from behind the counter and followed Ailia out to the wagon.

"Oh my, you weren't kidding when you said you had a lot. How did you get them to grow so big?" she asked as she picked up one of the tomatoes and looked at it, "this is almost as big as my head."

"I could never reveal my secrets," Ailia said with a shrug.

"Let's see here. How many eggs ya got?"

"Two dozen."

"And then each of your bushels are about twenty-five pounds right?"

"Yeah, I'd say."

"So two dozen eggs and twenty-five pound each of green long beans, tomatoes, carrots, turnips, beets, spring peas and potatoes for the veg right?"

"Yup, and then there are about thirty pounds of mixed berries. I have purple berries, black berries, and red berries."

"If you want to bring them in, I'll add up what I owe you. We'll take it all. No one else has had any decent harvest recently and certainly no one will ever bring me produce as big as yours. I really don't know how you do it."

Ailia nodded, smiling and grabbed the first bushel and carried it in behind the shop girl. Prudence directed her to the produce bins, and she went about filling them. As she worked, Prudence mumbled a few prices to herself, while writing down a few figures. Ailia made quick work of everything as Prudence did the math.

"All the produce is in. I'm just going to go grab the eggs, " she told Prudence. A few seconds later, Ailia set down the eggs in their basket, "So, what's my take?"

"I can give you a sapphire and a half per pound of vegetables. And you brought in a hundred seventy five pounds, which totals to nine emeralds and a half sapphire, then another one sapphire per pound for the berries and three more per dozen for the eggs… Which brings your total to half an amethyst, one emerald and twelve sapphires," Prudence said as she counted out the gemstones. "Is that all then today?"

"No, I need a sack of flour, some spirits, and herbs for canning. Also, I'm hoping you have a couple dozen canning jars today and hopefully I can order two or three more for pick up next week," Ailia answered as she put the gemstones in her hidden pouch and gazed around. Her eyes went to the fabric, and she walked over looking at the new calico. "How much is this pale yellow?"

Prudence put the sack of flour on the counter and looked up. "That's twenty-three sapphires a yard."

"Geez, I guess not today. I'll have to think about it. Maybe I can get some next month when I bring my canning in."

"Sounds good," Prudence said as she put the bottles of spirits on the counter.

Ailia grabbed the herbs she needed and took one last quick look around as Prudence went to the stockroom and grabbed two cases of jars.

"So what do I owe you?" Ailia as she set the herbs on the counter.

"Ahhh… Let me see," Prudence said as she counted up prices in her head, "twenty-one and half sapphires. I'll send your order out tomorrow and they should be here about this time next week."

Ailia nodded as she counted out the stones and handed them to Prudence before putting the flour on top of the cases of jars and grabbed them with one hand putting them on her hip. She grabbed the spirits and herbs with her other hand and walked out. She hurried out of the store nearly knocking Cara over.

Cara gasped, "Oh, sorry Ailia, didn't see you there."

Ailia smiled, "It is okay. I didn't see you either. How are you? It has been weeks."

"Great! Cedric and I just finished repairing the old Flaherty homestead out by Kiana's place."

"Well, that didn't take long. Have you been to see Kiana?"

Cara frowned. "Sadly no, I haven't been able to visit with the remodel."

Ailia nodded in agreement as Cedric came around the corner at a brisk pace, a heavy looking parcel under his arm.

"Oh, hello Ailia, I didn't know you'd be here."

"Garden is producing in buckets, plus we are low on flour and a few other things," Ailia shrugged, hefting the stack of goods under her arm. They walked over to Ailia's wagon.

"That's great," Cara replied. "With helping Cedric repair the house, I haven't had time for much more than a small garden. It may only be enough for the rainy season, but I'm hoping next growing season when it's calmer we will have a big garden again." Cara smiled and looked up at her husband who towered over her.

"Yes, next year we will be able to produce more." Cedric wrapped his arm around his wife's shoulders protectively and apologized, "Well, I hate to, but I have to steal Cara away. We have to finish up here in town and get back home to finish our final preparations for the storms."

"Oh, I understand completely," Ailia responded, and set her purchases down in the wagon before she hugged both of them. The pair waved good-bye and walked into the store.

"I will drop by next week sometime to catch up," Ailia called after them.

Cara turned and nodded. "I'm looking forward to it!"

As the door closed behind them, Ailia was distracted by a loud yelling coming from the center of town. She made sure Solas was still tightly tied before rushing towards the commotion.

Ailia tapped Old Man Boyd on the shoulder and asked, "What's going on here?"

"Some outsider said something to Seamus. I guess Seamus thinks he is Thren."

"Seamus thinks everyone is Thren, and he doesn't even believe in the Cosantóirí."

"Yes, dearie," The old man weakly shook his head and started to walk away.

"Thank you," Ailia called after him before making her way into the crowd.

She finally reached the edge of the crowd and saw a young man on his butt, covered in dust from the dirt road. He had muddy brown hair and weather worn skin. Seamus, the innkeeper, was standing over him, breathing, through his rusty brown whiskers as he clutched a bottle in his fist. The young man looked up at the innkeeper with no fear as he sprung into a crouch. Seamus flexed his knuckles with the rhythm of his breathing, turning them a pasty white as he took a step closer to the stranger.

"We don't like strangers," Seamus bellowed, breaking the bottle on a fence post before swinging it at him.

The young man stood, dodging the blow, "I didn't know," he said quietly looking Seamus in the eyes. "I was just looking for a bite to eat and a job. I am not trying to hurt anyone, I swear."

"That's not all ye wanted, scoundrel. I wouldn't take your word for nothing," Seamus yelled, swinging the bottle at the man's head. The man sidestepped him easily.

"It doesn't matter now," a voice shouted from the back of the crowd. Ailia tried to make out who said it but had no luck. A murmur started to spread through the crowd. A few villagers started to move towards the young man. As the crowd moved in closer the voices of the villagers grew louder and some became more pronounced. Several cried out for the stocks.

His eyes widened, and he trembled only once, fighting to keep his calm as he realized it was no longer just the innkeeper who was after him. Others began to move in closer and Ailia heard more of the villagers yell out.

"No stranger can be trusted," Sean shouted and moved closer to the man. As he advanced the villagers fed off the commotion and moved into a tighter circle.

Ailia felt for him and shouted out, "there is no need for violence."

Her plea got lost in the clamour of the crowd as they moved towards the young man. Ailia found it hard to make out what everyone was shouting but a few words like beat and kill hit her ears and knowing that this man didn't deserve mob justice for what was probably a simple miss underingstanding she tried to fight through the crowd but she could not get closer.

The crowd grew more and more violent and started to move in closer. They were almost to him when one of the village elders, the storyteller, in fact, strolled out from their midst and stood near the young man. Her face was creased with the stories of the past, and her red hair was speckled with silver and pulled back into a bun. Her piercing blue eyes shone with wisdom. No one knew her real name but she was called Kiana; just Kiana.

The stories she told made it seem like she had lived in Mynor for a thousand years, but she looked no older than anybody's grandma. When Ailia was younger she would come to town and sit in Kiana's living room just listening to stories with Cara for hours. Remembering this made Ailia's heart feel heavy with longing as

Kiana raised her right hand and tapped the ground with a knotted wooden staff.

Ailia thought. The crowd started to calm as Kiana's eyes seemed to penetrate their hearts.

"Are we all so suspicious that we will cause harm to an innocent young man?" her voice was light and airy yet strong. It floated on the wind to all present and the crowd quickly fell silent. "If we allow ourselves to harm this boy, we are no better than the Thren. We will not drop to their level. We must be better than that." "You're just an old hag. Why should we listen to you?" a young boy shouted.

Ailia looked in the direction of the voice and saw the youngest of the Byrnes boys, the village troublemakers. His mother, an orphan by the hands of the Thren, tried to hush him and when she couldn't, she took him by the arm and she dragged him home kicking and screaming.

Ailia shook her head and let a barely audible groan slip as she saw Sean Byrnes step out from the shadows of his butcher shop. She knew that he would agree with his son. Most of the villagers knew

this as well. They scowled at him as he took his boy's side.

"The boy is right," Sean yelled waving a butcher knife in the

air.

"Silence, Sean." Kiana paused and closed her eyes as if she

was seeing back in time. When she opened them again, her dark

blue irises steeled against the crowd. She continued as if Sean had

not spoken and instead answered his son's question. "You will listen

to me because you and everyone else in this town has always

listened to me and the other village elders." Kiana turned and looked

Sean in the eye. He shrank away from her, lowering his knife as

others pushed him to the back of the crowd.

"But he could be a Threnian." Seamus glared at the young

man while gripping the bottle he had broken earlier.

"I will find that out, as is my right being a village elder, but I

will do it on my own terms. There will be

violence here, Seamus." Kiana looked the portly man in the

eyes. He backed off, dropping the bottle harmlessly in the dirt.

Kiana turned to the young man. "Come with me."

He nodded softly as they walked towards her home and slowly the crowd dissipated.

She thought silently to herself as the villagers went back to their daily tasks. Ailia watched as Sean went back to his butcher shop and Seamus headed back into the inn. Soon the street was barren except for a few busy shoppers and a couple of old ladies gossiping. Ailia stood shocked at how quickly the villagers went from stark raving mad to calm as clams. She pondered this as she walked back to the market, mounted her wagon, and headed back to her farm. As she neared the edge of town she paused to look at the cloudless sky.

She thought

Her mind argued back,

Ailia blushed at her own thoughts and turned towards her home.

Chapter Three

Ailia hummed as she made her way home on the worn dirt
road. She looked around at the forest surrounding her and sighed,
wishing she could be among the familiar trees. Her humming made
her smile. The horse neighed in response to the song, and she got
lost in it. With her mind content to wander through the notes, Ailia
allowed her thoughts to become all consuming.

She had been on her way for several minutes and the town
had begun to disappear behind the mossy trees as the road bent. Ailia
knew the bend well and kept to the inside curve as she continued
because the outside curve was still torn up from last week's early
storm. As she rounded the corner, the young man from the village
pushed off from the tree and stood in her path.

Her horse reared, scared by a stranger and nearly toppled the
wagon. Ailia held firmly on the reins to steady the horse. When the
horse had calmed slightly she jumped down to calm her mare
further. She glared at the stranger. "What are you doing
here? Apparently you didn't cause enough ruckus in town? To think
I was trying to save you. I would almost think you are trying to get
me killed or worse my horse injured and wagon mangled. "

"Sorry, miss, I didn't mean anything by it. I didn't know your horse would spook."

Ailia rolled her eyes and sighed exasperated, "You still haven't answered my question."

He looked at her and said, "I'm Aiden. I'm trying to get some air away from the village. Things got pretty heated."

"Why did they?" she inquired as she continued to stroke her horse's neck.

"Seamus took something I said the wrong way, I guess. You're Ailia, aren't you?" Aiden asked.

"Um, did you say Aye-lee-ah?" she asked, trying to keep her face calm as she thought,

"So, it is your name then?"

Ailia looked at him blankly for a second before responding, "No, I just know you said it wrong. What did you say to Seamus anyway? You didn't ask about Thren did you?"

"Oh really, and how do you know that?" he countered, ignoring the Seamus comment.

"Why does it matter?"

"It doesn't really, miss, but just the same, I'd like to know how to say it right."

"Why should I tell you?" she inquired as she stroked Solas' mane.

He shrugged, "Curiosity."

"Um… okay I guess." Ailia rolled her eyes and shrugged. "If you really want to know, it's pronounced Ah-lee-ah."

"Let me get this right, Ah-lee-ah?"

"Yep, that's the name."

"So it is you?" Aiden asked with a hopeful note in his voice.

"I didn't say that"

"Do you know where I can find her? It's kinda important," He asked, kicking a rock on the road.

"Why is it so vital that you find her?"

"Well I was told that she might have a job for me."

"Really who told you that?"

"Kiana after she took me back to her place."

She pondered his intentions as she looked into his warm brown and gold flecked eyes. They burned with a strong kindness she couldn't fathom she would ever see in a Threnian's eyes.

she concluded as she smiled at him and murmured, "Okay fine, I suppose you're harmless enough. I am Ailia."

He sighed and smiled a charming crooked half smile as she took a closer look at him. The sun danced off the natural brown highlights in his pitch black hair as the wind blew softly through it. It was slightly unruly, but it gave his features a playful edge to their serious nature. The light stubble on his chin highlighted his strong jaw and added years to his somewhat boyish face. His dirt-colored clothes and worn shoes had red clay speckled over them. Both of his pant legs had patches over his knees.

She looked him over and shrugged. Ailia decided not to bother with him any longer.

she thought as she patted her horse before mounting the wagon without a second thought and snapped the reins to spur Solas forward.

"Wait, Ailia," he called out to her before she could leave him on the side of the road.

She paused and let the reins slack, slowing to a stop only a few feet from where she started. She turned in the seat and looked at him, rolling her eyes. "What?"

"I'm going to be sticking around this area for a while and looking for work. Like I said Kiana thought you might need a farm hand."

"I can't help you. I have to get home."

Aiden looked around and when he didn't see or hear anyone, he leaned towards her and asked, "You can't even pause to help a fellow Cosantóirí?"

Ailia answered in a soft hiss, "You're a member? I don't believe you. You're just saying that because you think it will matter to me. Like I said I don't have time for this."

Aiden took off a bracelet and tossed it up to her. Ailia caught it and examined the brown leather set with small red stones. The sun hit the stones and they sparkled in her eyes. She tossed the bracelet back to Aiden.

"I don't know who you think you are and I don't care. A bit of leather doesn't mean a thing and won't change anything either. I don't have time for this nonsense. I have a farm to tend to."

"I can help out. Like I said, I'm looking for work."

"Well, I'm not looking for a worker, and I don't need the hassle of making sure you do your work correctly. So scram, you're wasting my time."

With that remark, Ailia snapped the reins of the wagon and urged her wagon for home, leaving Aiden standing in the dust of the road, calling her name. Ailia fumed on the way home, muttering as she led the wagon down the dirt road. When Ailia reached the farm, she pulled the wagon under its basic thatched covering and hopped down to unhitch Solas.

As she led her horse into the stables and took off her bridle, Ailia thought she could hear her father speaking with someone but ignored it and got straight to work. She hung the bridle up on the tack wall in the supplies room and walked back to the wagon and began to unpack the purchases. She carried them inside and put the jars on the counter to tackle what canning she could tomorrow and then took the rest of the purchases down to the cellar to store them. When she came back upstairs she saw her father speaking to someone out by the barn. She went back to the barn and spent the next hour or so tending to the horses.

When she walked back to the house, her father was still talking to the same person. She couldn't quite make out who it was from the porch so Ailia went out to investigate.

As she moved closer, she realized her father was speaking with Aiden and glared at him, each step making her angrier.

Fuming, she stopped in front of Aiden and yelled at him, "What do you think you're doing here? I told you I wasn't interested in a farm hand."

Waylin cleared his throat stopping her rant in its tracks. He turned from Aiden for a moment and Ailia dropped her gaze to the ground biting her tongue.

"That's no way to talk to our new hand, Ailia. Where are your manners, girl?" Waylin snapped at her with his eyes steeled in her direction. She could see him forming a fist.

"Of course, Father," She bowed her head slightly, then looked at Aiden and through gritted teeth and softly apologized.

"That's better. Now I have noticed that the farm is getting run down. I've hired Aiden here at fifteen sapphires a week. You'll be in charge of making sure he earns it, if you can handle that. I don't want to hear any gripping on your part, either. We are coming to the rainy season and the buildings are unacceptable, stupid girl,"

He sneered before continuing, "We need better structures and you're

incapable of doing it yourself. I don't want to have to clean up

another mess like last rainy season."

Waylin turned to Aiden. "You start right now. There is at

least a couple good hours of sunlight left. I have things to tend to in

the workshop. If she gives you any more trouble just let me know.

I'll deal with her." Waylin had started to walk away and then he

turned back and said. "Oh, as long as you're working for us, you can

sleep in the barn loft and we will provide your meals. See you for

breakfast."

Waylin turned and retreated into his workshop muttering and

Ailia scowled at Aiden. After her father had moved from earshot,

she shrugged and stared at him, still fuming. "Well, since I'm forced

to put up with you, let's get one thing straight. I'm the boss, and you

do what I say. Got it?"

"Got it," Aiden hastily responded.

"Have you ever worked on a farm before?" Aiden shook his

head and Ailia sighed. "Well then, we will start with the chickens.

They are all out in the yard right now, so it's the perfect time for you to clean their coop."

Ailia gestured to Aiden to follow, leading him to the supply room. She showed him the pile of clean hay in the corner of the room and then the compost heap on the far right side of the barn. Handing Aiden a rake and bucket, she told him to clean the soiled hay and line the coop with fresh. Satisfied even he couldn't mess up that job, she headed in to brush down the horses without giving Aiden another thought.

He took the bucket and the rake and headed to the hen house. He opened the door, and crinkled up his nose before getting to work scraping all of the soiled hay into the bucket. It took him a few trips back and forth to the compost heap and awhile but when he was done he sent the empty bucket down outside the barn and went back inside to grab the fresh hay. Aiden laid the hay down on the floor of the hen house in neat layers and then proceeded to fill the chickens' water. When it was looking as good as he thought it could Aiden grabbed the empty bucket and went to find Ailia.

Ailia sighed and brushed down Solas. The repetitive strokes of the brush against her mare's muscled body calmed Ailia. She lost track of time until she heard a faint knock on the gate of the stable. She whipped her head up and saw Aiden leaning against the wood frame of the door.

"What's next, boss?" he asked, shrugging his shoulders.

"The horses' stalls need to be cleaned and fresh hay put down as well. I'll move the horses out to the pen to give you room. After you're through changing the hay, you can get them clean water from the well and put fresh oats in their feed bins. The oats are in the supply room after that you can go for the night. There should be enough in there for today. I'll show you where to fill the barrel tomorrow. Be back here right after sunrise in the morning, and I advise you to eat before you come. You're only going to get lunch from me and don't be late."

"Wait, your father said breakfast too. If I'm staying here, won't I be with you all three meals?" Aiden asked standing up and putting his hands in his pockets.

"I suppose you're right but that doesnt mean I have to like it." Ailia stated.

"Do you want me to lead them back into their pens too?" Aiden asked after a brief silence.

"No, I'll do that. They aren't used to strangers; I'd rather not have to dig a grave for you if they trample you to death. When you're done with the horses' stalls grab two buckets from the turnip bin and feed the pigs. Now, if you don't mind, I have other things I have to do."

Aiden nodded once and headed to the supply room to grab the larger rake for the stalls. Ailia led each horse out one by one to the pen to graze and relax, then checked to make sure the chickens had fresh water. To her surprise, Aiden had already filled it. Ailia smiled and rounded up the hens, funneling them one by one into their freshly cleaned house for the night and dropped the wooden latch.

She checked on Aiden and found that he had finished with Solas's stall and moved on to the stallion, Iasair's. She called Solas over to her and led her back to her stall. As she secured the stall door shut, Ailia sighed.

She moved the horses back for the night one by one, continuing her internal rant. When the last horse was safe in their stall Ailia found Aiden outside sitting against the barn staring at the dusky sky. She informed him supper would be on the table shortly.

"Okay," he responded, not really paying attention. Ailia had started to turn back to the house when suddenly Aiden spoke again, "I was wondering if you could show me where I'll be sleeping. I'm more tired than hungry so… kinda just want to bed down for the night."

"I don't know if I am overly fond of this arrangement, but follow me, I guess,"Ailia said and gestured for him to follow. She walked into the barn and led Aiden to the right side of the supply room where a ladder stood partially hidden.

"Well, I'll leave you here. There is some hay up there to make a bed. I should say come find me if you need anything, but," she paused for a mere second, "don't."

Chapter Four

The sun rose and woke Ailia; she put on her work clothes and walked out to her farm. Aiden was waiting for her by the barn looking bright eyed and cocky with a half grin on his face.

"You're prompt I'll give you that," Ailia remarked as she approached him.

"You did say daylight, Boss and it's not as if I have far to walk," Aiden snickered.

"That was rhetorical, wisecrack. So first off this morning, I'm going to lay down some ground rules. Rule number one: Knock that 'boss' shit off right now. It makes you sound condescending. It also annoys me." Ailia paused and waited for Aiden to acknowledge her and he obliged.

"Rule number two: Don't get in my way. I didn't want you here in the first place. You have no experience and will be more trouble than you're worth," Ailia continued her voice sharpening, "Rule number three: Do it right the first time. That applies to whatever I happen to tell you to do. I'm not going to be happy if I have to go back and correct your work . And lastly rule number four: I don't like you."

Aiden nodded and waited with his hands in his pockets

before saying, "Well it's a good thing your father does."

Ailia rolled her eyes at him and ignored the comment. She

motioned for him to follow her and walked closer to the field.

"Now that we have that straight, let's get to work." She

pointed to the field and told Aiden to start weeding. "I'll ring the bell

when breakfast is ready."

Aiden nodded and began. Ailia left him to his task and went to

collect the fresh eggs from the hen house and prepared breakfast just

like every other ordinary day. Except today she made one extra

plate.

The four ate in silence and when everyone was finished Ailia

stood and readied the wash bin. Waylin and Rhona shuffled out of

the kitchen and she grabbed the dishes to wash them.

"Stop twiddling your thumbs and go back to work," she

snapped at Aiden as he coughed.

"Yes, boss," He quickly responded and left before she could

say another word. He went back to work as Ailia finished the dishes.

After she had them dried and put away, Ailia headed out to the well

and pulled up a bucket of water. She brought it into the kitchen and fetched a few turnips, carrots, and potatoes from the cellar. She cleaned and diced them before putting a pot on to boil and adding them in. Ailia put the pot on a bed of warm coals away from the direct heat.

She left them to cook and went out to the farm where she found Aiden still weeding leaving a mess of pulled dead vegetation everywhere.

"What do you think you're doing?"

"Weeding..." Aiden stuttered, caught off guard by her sharp voice. "You asked me to do this."

"I wasn't referring to that. I was talking about these messy piles of dead things all over my farm."

"Oh... I wasn't sure where you wanted me to do with them. Sorry."

Ailia shook her head but didn't respond. Instead, she began to inspect his work. Her expression never changed as she walked among the rows of plants but her thoughts did.

Ailia shrugged and gestured for him to follow. She led him to the other side of the barn where a large woodpile was located.

"I know you're not done weeding and you're nowhere near done cleaning up the weeds but I wanted to show you your next task. I need you to split the smaller logs so we can build the new structures. Leave the long ones alone. I need the whole pile done. I'd like to inform you that despite what my father may think of me, I run a tidy farm. I like it that way so I expect your work area to remain tidy no matter what you're doing." Ailia paused and Aiden nodded his head in acknowledgment. "As for the piles of weeds, you know where the compost is. I suggest you utilize it. Now I have my own tasks to accomplish. I trust you can manage the tasks I gave you. Don't make more work for me."

He nodded again and headed back to the field. She watched him for a few seconds before going to the barn and leading the horses out to their grazing pen. She closed the latch on the gate to the pasture and walked back into the barn and went into the supply room. She pulled a belt off the wall and fastened it around her waist, her hatchet into one of the loops on her left side and putting her clippers in the other one. Ailia grabbed a woven basket that stood about waist high and attached a strap to it before flinging it over her shoulder and resting it in between her shoulder blades. She double checked the strap and her belt to make sure they were secure before heading out into the forest in search of fallen branches.

Ailia walked through the woods looking for any suitable building materials. When she did come across a branch she would use her axe to trim off the thicker side branches and her clippers for the thin ones. When they were clean of any side branches she would put them in her basket. She grabbed branches of all lengths and various thicknesses to make sure the roof and side walls had strong flexible support. Ailia spent a good part of the morning filling the basket several times over.

Each time she would take a quick jog back to the farm and dump the load near to where Aiden was cutting wood. After the first load, Ailia noticed he took his shirt off and the sweat glistened from his body. She also noticed that while he had some definition in his muscle groups she suspected he had not spent his life doing hard labor.

When her basket was full for the fourth time, she continued picking up branches until her arms were full as well. She turned for home and when Ailia neared her farm again she could still hear the swing of the axe and the grunts of Aiden's efforts lingering in the air as she dropped the last of her finds in the pile.

She appeared in front of him and asked, "How's it going?"

Aiden jerked his head up, "Oh, I'm almost finished. Looks like you were busy as well."

"I'm always busy." Ailia said simply. When he didn't say anything back and continued to chop wood, she sighed and set her basket down. "Well, seeing as you're almost done and it's nearly midday why don't you finish up and put your shirt back on and then come into the house for lunch, which I must go finish now."

Aiden nodded and grabbed another log as Ailia left and walked back to the house. She headed down to the cellar pulling some cured meat out to add to the soup she had started earlier. As she climbed up the stairs, she ran through the plans for the new structure.

Her thoughts continued as she cubed up the meat and added into the bubbling pot. As it boiled Ailia started to wipe down the counters and Aiden walked in from the chopping block all grimed up and sweaty. Without looking at him Ailia told him that there was a wash bin in the corner.

After he had washed his hands and face she grabbed a bucket and pushed the scraps of meat and vegetable scraps into it before handing it to Aiden.

"Take this to the chickens," Ailia ordered him

Aiden nodded, taking the bucket and walked it out to the chicken coop and flung the scraps around for the chickens to pick at. He returned to the kitchen, put the bucket away, and stood out of Ailia's way. She stirred the soup and without missing a beat, she pointed to a chair. Aiden took this as a command to sit which he ignored and stood by the wall. She rolled her eyes and ignored him. Five minutes later Ailia sliced a loaf of bread and rang the dinner bell.

While they waited for Rhona to appear from one of her many spirit induced naps and Waylin to emerge from his workshop, Ailia grabbed 4 bowls and set the table with them. Once everyone was seated, she dished out the soup and set the slices of bread out. Finally she sat down. Silence crept over them and just when Ailia thought that this would pass as most other meals, Aiden started talking.

"So Waylin, how long have you been settled here?"

Ailia grimaced and braced herself for her father's yelling but instead he smirked and said, "oh we have been here for nearly sixteen years I think now. We came here when Ailia was just a babe,"

"Well you have a beautiful home," Aiden said looking around the bare room. Ailia thought she noticed a bit of sarcasm in his voice but thankfully Waylin didn't.

"Thank you Aiden. Maybe with your help we can spruce it up even more. My daughter can't handle this by herself. She's really not all that bright. Most days I'm surprised she can even manage what we have."

Ailia bit her lip and wanted to say something but she knew better.

she thought and much to her relief Aiden did not say anything further. Her father finished first. He stood and shuffled to the front door and walked back to the workshop. Rhona followed him out stumbling into the barn and Ailia stood collecting the dirty dishes. She walked out of the house to the well. Aiden followed. Ailia started to crank the well and bring up the bucket.

Aiden took her hand and said, "Here let me do that for you,"
He paused, "I am sorry about..... ya know"

Ailia looked at him with her mouth slack. After a short pause she nodded, mumbled something and backed away letting Aiden assist her. When he had pulled up the bucket, he carried it to the house for her. She stood by the well frozen for a few more seconds. Her mind torn trying to decide to say something stupid or to just appreciate that she didn't have to do it all herself this time.

A chicken walked by Ailia and clucked startling her back to reality. She shook her head a few times and walked into the house. She looked around and saw the bucket on the counter next to Aiden. Ailia warmed the water he had carried in and looked at him. "You can go wait for me by the wood pile, I won't be more than five minutes."

He nodded and walked out as she plunged the first dish into the almost boiling water.

It wasn't long before Ailia was heading out to meet him, rolling up her sleeves.

"Let's get to work. I want the basic structure done before dusk. We also have to tend to the animals before we turn in."

The two worked together in silence, only speaking when necessary for the rest of the afternoon. First Ailia sent Aiden to the supply room for shovels and they dug holes at the four corners of the new storage area for the wagon. She also had him dig a spot for a mid post on each wall. In these spots the two of them worked together to hoist and slide the longer logs into them. Ailia then went to the barn and grabbed several lengths of ropes and several other tools so they could begin to latch the smaller logs Aiden had chopped.

They stood the logs vertically, one next to the other, in between each of the taller logs. When the first section was done, Ailia took one of the ropes and weaved it across the midpoint of the smaller logs along the side of one wall.

"While I work on the rope can you please continue on with the logs?" Ailia asked.

"Yeah, of course." Aiden continued to place the logs and after a while. He paused, "Ailia, I don't agree with your father, by the way. You are very bright. I could have never figured out how to build a structure."

She looked up at him from where she knelt, "I understand that you didn't mean anything by it but I would rather not talk about what happened. If you don't mind."

Aiden nodded and continued to place the short logs vertical. They worked in unison until the rope was running up and down both walls of the structure. Ailia then took the smaller branches she had gathered and began to stuff them in and loose places in the wall.

"Do you want me to start at the other end doing that?" He asked. Ailia nodded and he copied her direction and quickly they had the bottom half of the wall stable and moved up to the top half. After securing a thick horizontal log across each portion of the wall the pair built the top half of the wall in much the same fashion.

Once the walls had the first step finished they took the remaining branches Ailia had gathered and using some fine twine she tied the ends together to make panels for the roof. They rested these against the walls just as the sun began to sink below the trees, Ailia wiped her hands on her pants and took a step back to survey their work. She smiled at the bones of her new structure.

"I'm satisfied for tonight; tomorrow we will go in search of thatch for the roof."

"Understood," Aiden responded before asking. "Are you done with me for the day?"

"No, I need you to round up the chickens back to the coop for the night. I will take care of the rest of the animals."

"After that do you mind if I head into town then?"

"As long as you don't cause another ruckus, I don't mind," Ailia said as she tidied up the work area.

"I didn't plan on the first one and I don't plan on a second either. I just promised Kiana I'd check in."

Ailia nodded and stared up at the sky as Aiden went to gather the chickens. He left quietly after and walked into town. As the first stars began to twinkle Ailia decided that tomorrow while Aiden was working she would go and see Cara and Kiana.

She finished bedding down the animals and retired to her room, lapsing into a fitful sleep. Birds chirped and leaves rustled as she ran free. She stopped to catch her breath. A soft giggle escaped her lips as she viewed the spring forest and the new life teeming within the trees. A loud noise erupted behind her. The forest disappeared and all was dark except a floating figure with the likeness of Aiden coming towards her.

"Really, even my dreams?" she yelled at him.

He floated around her, not saying a word, just tormenting her, his form only half solid. She stumbled away, tripping over a rock. She picked it up. He smiled his cocky half smile and she pitched the rock at him. It sailed through him and smacked something hard in the dark. It was like he was made of smoke from a tainted fire. His hand reached out to her and she could feel the air brush her cheek. She took a step back but he followed. Her heart raced faster as she scrambled backward, he pursued her at an even pace until she reached a cliff. Without knowing she stepped off of it and was plunged into the abyss below. Aiden's face staring at her the whole way down, his hand outstretched.

※ ※ ※ ※ ※ ※

Aiden knocked on Kiana's door. He heard the creak of a rocking chair and moments later the door opened.

"Come in, Aiden," Kiana said

He nodded and walked into the living room. "Drink?" asked Kiana.

"Yeah, that would be great."

Kiana walked into the kitchen and Aiden stirred the fire. The smoke rose up and formed a picture of Ailia, her hair flowing out around the image.

"Dreaming again, I see," Kiana said, walking into the room with a tray of biscuits and steaming tea. Aiden jumped, the image of Ailia disappearing into the air. He turned and looked at her, "No I was just stirring the fire."

"Ah, so how goes it as a farm hand," Kiana said, giving him a knowing glance.

"Ailia is a hard boss. I don't think she likes me much or trusts me, since I had to go overhead to stay close to her."

Kiana nodded and smiled. "I expected as much. This will be no easy task."

Aiden nodded and took a sip of his tea. "Do you have any suggestions?"

"Earning her trust, child, is key. Ailia doesn't really know what it is to be cared for by another. She has always had to do everything herself. Waylin isn't a kind man and how he has raised that child will only make your mission harder. She will resist with every fiber of her being because she is able to sense you bring great change. That is something that scares her more than anything. If you remain loyal, considerate and someone she can depend on, the winds of fortune may smile on this mission yet."

"That's little comfort, but I always knew this mission would not be a quick one."

"Aye," Kiana sipped her tea and took a few moments to think before continuing, "It doesn't help that we live in uncertain times. I have done what I can to guide her, and I will continue to do so when she comes to me to seek advice, but I can't tell her what to do. The rest is up to her and those, that fate dictates, around her."

The pair sat in silence for a few minutes enjoying the warm tea as a contrast to the cool night breeze filling the room from the open window. Aiden took the last sip of his and grabbed a purple berry biscuit, taking a bite of it as he stood and walked to the window.

He swallowed and turned towards Kiana asking, "Are we doing the right thing taking everything from her like this?"

Kiana stood and walked to the window, she placed a hand on Aiden's shoulder and murmured, "What other choice do we have?"

Aiden sighed, "If she thinks she hates me now, I can't imagine how much she will really hate me after the truth comes out."

"Don't fret my child. You're too young to give yourself wrinkles. Leave that pleasure to me, dearie."

Aiden nodded and the two stood at the window watching the stars begin to sparkle in the night sky .The moon rose to midpoint.

Kiana turned to Aiden. "The hour is late, child. You're more than welcome to stay, but I must retire now."

"I appreciate your offer, but Waylin offered me the barn loft. So I bid you a good night, Kiana. I will check back in a few days."

"Until then, my child, keep your chin up." Kiana nodded and disappeared down the hallway.

Aiden extinguished the fire and left the house in silence. He looked at the town path and then at the forest. Aiden walked into the woods. He took his time exploring the path that led northeast towards the farmstead. He let his mind go blank as he familiarized himself with the trees and the scampering animals. He took his time going through the forest and arrived back at Ailia's farm as the sky faded from blackened navy to a dusky mauve. Though he had not gotten any sleep during the night he felt rested and ready for

whatever Ailia decided to throw at him today.

Chapter Five

When Ailia awoke early the next morning she was slightly
sore from the hard work of yesterday and troubled by her dreams the
night before. She stood and stretched her muscles before getting
dressed, trying to be energized and hopeful. She took a deep breath.

She went outside and started her morning routine, eager to
be done with it. She went out to the chicken coop and opened the
door. As the chickens scampered out, she noticed, so did the farms'
roosters. Knowing that they had not missed an opportunity she let
out a low scream. Ailia, with an ever growing anger, marched to the
barn and up the ladder to wake Aiden only to find him unaccounted
for.

She went about the rest of her morning routine fuming that
he had not yet shown up and that he had let the rooster in the hen
house.

After she had collected the eggs she went to the feed room to
collect the scraps for the chickens. She spotted Aiden walking out of
the barn, yawning.

"Where were you?" Ailia asked when she had emptied the
bucket.

"What do you mean, I just woke up."

"You are a liar and I will not stand for it."

Aiden sighed, "Fine. I spent the night in the woods exploring the land after I left Kiana's place. Why does it matter? It's not that far past daylight and I'm here now."

"Normally, I wouldn't really care, especially since I'm not fond of you staying here anyway, but it matters because you messed up big time and now there is extra work to be done. Work you have to do." Ailia told him, her eyes boring deeper into him with each word.

"What did I do wrong?" Aiden asked, taking a slight step back from her.

Ailia pointed to the nearest chicken and said, "This is a hen it lays eggs. Eggs that will never become baby chicks." She pointed to the rooster. "That is a rooster. His job is to protect the girls and, if he gets the chance, make baby chicks with them. Now I sell eggs,

eggs, as part of what helps this farm stay afloat. We also eat them."

"I understand all of that."

"I highly doubt that, considering when I opened the hen house this morning, Mister Rooster and his buddies strode out in all of his glory."

"Why is that a bad thing?" Aiden asked.

Ailia took a deep breath and called him a few names in her head before continuing, "In a week's time I will lose each and every egg those hens lay for a week. That's over a hundred eggs that I have to put in a warmer and nurture until they hatch or go in the compost."

Ailia let that soak in for a moment as Aiden's eyes grew a little bit wider. Realizing what he had done, he started to speak and Ailia cut him off.

"Sorry won't fix this. Your only saving grace is that I was going to try for new chicks after the monsoon season has passed us by. And the ones I don't want I should be able to sell. So it's not a total loss, just a lot of work that you're going to have to do."

"I understand. So what's the first thing that needs to be done?

"Well, first off we are going to need more building materials. I am going into town to buy what I can today. The rest will have to be ordered in. While I am in town I need you to go into the woods and gather as many tall grasses and reeds as you can find. Even willow branches will do. The basket I used the other day for the sticks is in the supply room. There is also a pair of clippers in there or feel free to use your knife."

Ailia paused for Aiden to nod. He did so and she continued, "To the south of the farm there is a river and some marshland. That should be a good place to start your search. I don't want anything shorter than two feet, so leave the shorter ones to keep growing. We may need to do a second harvest. I want you to fill at least half a dozen crates with the thatch. The crates are down underneath the loft."

"Will do. Again, I am sorry, I had no idea it would be this much work."

"Save it. Sorry won't change the work you have to do. Just make sure that tonight the roosters are in the barn, not the hen house. I have to make breakfast now. Tend to the other animals."

"I'll get them taken care of and I will be doubly sure the roosters are far from the hens from now on."

Aiden went to the feed shed and Ailia to the kitchen. She made quick work of cooking eggs and adding fresh vegetables. Ailia rang the dinner bell and everyone assembled. As they sat and ate she mulled around how to tell her father.

Finally she cleared her throat, "So in six days we will start incubating eggs for about a week."

Waylin swallowed hard and looked at his daughter, "Girl, how could you be so blasted stupid." He slammed his hand down on the table and his voice grew louder, " How many times have I told you to keep the damn roosters out of the hen house at night?"

"This was done on purpose. Our hens are slowing down. We need fresh young chickens to help keep up."

Her father stood and pushed the plates off the table and shouted, "Learn your place. I'll tell you when we need new chickens. You insolent child, this is my farm and I'm the decision maker. Don't think of doing something like this ever again."

Aiden cleared his throat to speak but from the corner of his eye he saw Ailia shake her head no. Her face was flushed, but she softly apologized to her father. It seemed to calm him slightly. Waylin left the table with a grunt and a slam of the door as he headed back out to his workshop. Rhona was next as she stumbled back to her bedroom. Then Aiden stood and left as well. Ailia stared at the table, angry tears spilling from her eyes for a few moments. She wiped them when she heard someone coming to the door. She stood and gathered the dishes from the floor and set them on the counter. She picked up the food from the floor and put it into a bucket with the egg shells and vegetable scraps. The front door opened and Aiden walked in with a bucket of water for her. As he set the bucket down next to Ailia he could tell that she had shed a few tears.

He wanted to comfort her but didn't know what to say so instead he asked, "Why did you take the blame?"

"It was a calculated risk. There was a chance he wouldn't get mad if I said it was deliberate, or well, I had hoped for that at least. It would have been worse if it was your mistake." She told him as she started the dishes.

"I could have handled it."

"You mistake me, I wasn't trying to protect you in the least. He wouldn't have been mad at you. You're my responsibility. Therefore anything you do wrong is doubly bad as a reflection on my leadership and apparent carelessness on my part."

Ailia looked at him, and, for the first time, Aiden saw her vulnerable,almost meek. Like the spirit had been torn from her by force. He could see years of pain swirl in her emerald green eyes and after what he had witnessed he understood why. It only lasted for a mere second before she turned back to her work. He lingered still trying to find something else to say to make it better.

He was still thinking when she turned back to him again. Her demeanor had steeled once more and she told him to get back to work. He nodded and left quietly to go about collecting the thatch. She quickly finished the last of the dishes and dumped the dirty water. She then changed her clothes and left Rhona a note telling her there was some jar soup in the cellar for lunch and that she was headed into town.

Ailia quickly saddled Solas and rode into town. Her first stop was Prudence. It didn't take her long to purchase the amount of rope she needed and two lots of hay to be delivered directly to the farm early next week. Ailia also bought several spools of fine twine. Once she had made her purchases Ailia informed Prudence about the chicks that would be for sale in a month and a half and also that subsequently there would be no eggs from her farm for a bit.

Prudence put a note on the bulletin board and helped Ailia carry her wares out to Solas. They loaded her saddle bags and then Ailia was off to see Cara. She made it to Cara's before the sun had reached its peak and knocked on the front door.

"Ailia, this is a surprise! What brings you here?" Cara asked when she opened the front door to see her best friend on her porch.

"Told ya I would be coming by didn't I?"

"Well yes but I didn't expect you for another few days at least."

"Can I come in anyway?" Ailia asked with a shrug.

"Oh of course, where are my manners," Cara chuckled and wiped her hands on her apron before leading her inside, "I'll put on a kettle to boil and we'll have ourselves a bit of tea."

"I love the place," Ailia mused as she admired Cedric's fine carving of the kitchen archway.

"It would be half as pretty without that dear man of mine. You know, now that I am all settled and such, we really should find you a man." Cara rattled on as she put the kettle on and dusted off the already clean kitchen table.

"I don't think so. I'm perfectly happy where I am at right now. Besides you snagged the last eligible bachelor for three towns on either side of Latzu," Ailia joked as she sat at the table.

"I wouldn't say that. Besides, I've noticed that the handsome stranger seems to be sticking around. Kiana seems fond enough of him. Maybe you could snag him up and get him some roots."

"I will have nothing to do with that man. At least if I can help it. I doubt that will be possible." Ailia said through gritted teeth just as the kettle whistled.

"Geez Ailia, what's with you?" she asked, as she busied herself around the kitchen, grabbing cups and serving tea.

"Sorry," Ailia stirred her tea, her posture relaxing, "He just really bugs me. He asked me for work and I told him no so he talked to my father. Now he is our farm hand. To top it off Pa gave him the barn loft."

"That's cute, he must be smitten with you, I'm sure of it now. What's his name again?"

Ailia gritted her teeth and refused to answer but Cara asked again and she blurted out, "Aiden, though I wish I could forget it."

"Well you know what they say about proximity." Cara chuckled, swirling her tea about.

"It breeds contempt? I mean he is a blundering idiot."

"He can't be that bad? Can he?"

Ailia rolled her eyes and took a sip of her tea before saying, "He let the roosters in the hen house last night."

"Well…," Cara paused, "At least he is cute." She shrugged her shoulders and smiled.

"Not even that will save him. I mean if it were up to me."

"Well I wouldn't give up on him just yet. I mean if I were you, that is."

"Cara, you know a relationship is not in the cards for me, at least not right now. There just isn't enough time to care for the farm, the animals and make sure dad's happy and mom doesn't burn the house down when she's drunk. You have seen them first hand," Ailia paused and took a sip of tea, "Maybe if things calm down someday I might think about it, but it won't be Aiden. I can promise you that."

"Ailia, you're right. I know all of the reasons you have never taken a serious look at any relationship, but I think that's exactly why you need someone who makes you the priority."

"Enough, Cara." Ailia stirred her tea and shrugged.

They sat in silence, drinking tea for a few minutes. Cara smiled and said, "Hey, I know what will cheer you up. Let's go see Kiana. I have some news for both of you."

"Really now, do I get a sneak preview?" Ailia asked, sipping her tea.

"Not a chance," Cara laughed.

"That's not fair. Why'd you tell me that you have news if you aren't going to tell me what it is?" Ailia whined.

Cara chuckled and sipped her tea, "The faster you finish your drink the faster we can go over to Kiana's."

Ailia took one last gulp of the hot tea and smiled, "I'm done."

Cara laughed as she picked up the cups and thoroughly rinsed them.

"Those can dry while we are gone," she said, turning them upside down upon a towel before grabbing her bonnet.

The pair walked outside and Ailia untied Solas's reins. The group walked into the whipping wind and tightened their shawls as they took a short walk along the lake shore to Kiana's home. Cara knocked as Ailia tied up Solas. Kiana ushered them in.

"What brings you ladies here?" Kiana asked as the pair slipped off their shawls and hung them by the door. Ailia stirred up the fire and gently added another log into its hungry maw. The fire licked at the wood, coaxing out its moisture with hisses and crackles as the girls warmed from their brief walk.

"Seeing you in town rescuing Aiden made me realize how much I missed our visits. I miss your stories and the homemade bread, all of it."

"I'm with Ailia on the bread."

"You girls are so predictable you know that. I put the bread in the oven right before you got here. What story should I tell this time around?" Kiana asked,as she poured herself a cup of tea and sat in the rocking chair.

Reverting to younger versions of themselves they shouted out in unison a single word, 'Daoine'. Kiana laughed as both girls sat cross-legged in front of her like they were five years old again.

"Like I said, predictable. This story starts with three brothers. They were quite young and lived with their mother in a small cabin in the northernmost part of Mynor past the farthest mountain range. They spent most of the year inside because a deep darkness had fallen over the land and monsters roamed the woods.

"Now these boys were special, for they were the last of their race. You see they weren't human even though they looked like any of us. They were Daoine. The Daoine people are an old race of immortal beings. They were not immortal like the fae because they could be killed but time and sickness did not touch them. Centuries before our three brothers were born, the Daoine were a plentiful race that speckled every inch of Mynor. Their cities were known as places for knowledge and industry. Sadly, those cities were not meant to last. A war had broken out between the Daoine and the Scáth. Like the witch hunters of late, the Scáth hunted the Daoine until it was believed that only five were left in existence," Kiana paused and took a long sip of her tea before continuing.

"The Daoine did fight back and the Scáth lost just as much. When the last of the Scáth came for the remaining Daoine the battle was bloody. The father of the three boys took many hits but with the last of his life force decimated all of the attackers. The blows dealt by the Scáth were too much for him however and the father passed into the void leaving his wife to raise their three boys alone.

"Years later, when these three boys were about to come into their Magick powers. It would happen during the course of the summer, which was very short indeed where they lived. The main topic of conversation most days was of course what Magick powers they would be blessed with. Two of the boys were saddened by the loss of their father, but they had moved on and were able to look to the future. They talked about wanting to do good with whatever Magick the fae gifted them with. Their brother, however, could not move past the terrible blow and thought of avenging his father's death.

"As time passed, darkness crept into the boy's heart of hearts. The darkness started small, with little things like an uncalled for push or shove as the boys played. By the time the boys grew into men, the mother could no longer ignore what had become of her son.

It scared her, and unsure what to do, she held counsel with the fae about her son as they were the ones to decide which son would receive which power. You see Daoines were not born with power but rather given power because of their long lifespan.

"The fae watched the young man and they saw the darkness too. They knew he could be dangerous with Magick so at the end of the summer they denied him Magick and blessed his brothers with formidable gifts. This outraged the youngest of the sons. Within weeks he left home. Upon his departure, he swore to exact his revenge on all mankind and Magick kind for he felt slighted. The darkness in his heart wouldn't let him see the truth. It consumed him and soon he became nothing more than pure evil. That's where the story fades into the unknown. Some say that his two brothers killed him or locked him up. Others say that he killed them. I'd like to believe that they are all still alive."

"Did he exact his revenge first?" Cara asked, interrupting.

"Well, some say that his brothers did nothing and that he still lives and still plots, though no one knows for sure if he is still in existence or not."

"So the moral of the story is that you shouldn't let darkness inside your heart."

"The moral of the story is what you take from it." Kiana sniffed the air, "Bread's done who wants some?"

They both answered yes and followed Kiana to the kitchen. She took the fresh loaf out of the oven and placed it on the wooden counter. Using a sharp knife she cut off four slices. As she was handing them out Aiden walked in the back door.

"Fresh bread, Aiden?" Kiana asked, offering him the fourth slice.

"Please, I spent most of the morning gathering thatch for the farm." He turned to Ailia, "I gathered what you asked for and heated up lunch for Rhona and Waylin. I wasn't sure what you wanted after that so I came to town searching for you."

"Great, I didn't expect it to take so long in town." Ailia responded and took a bite of her bread.

"Yes, it is getting later in the day," Kiana mused.

Cara looked out the window, "And I haven't even told you my good news yet. I won't keep you waiting any longer, especially with the storm coming."

"You and Cedric are expecting," Kiana whispered softly as she hugged Cara.

"Your powers of deduction never stop amazing me. The doctor confirmed it yesterday."

Ailia hugged her friend and started to cry. "This is so amazing!"

Aiden saw her face come alive with joy and, not wanting to ruin the moment, excused himself, nodding softly to Kiana. She acknowledged him and clasped Cara's shoulder joining the girls in their celebration. After a few minutes of crying and laughing the girls calmed down.

"Well, I hate to leave you guys but I really should go start supper for Cedric and I," Cara sighed and put on her shall. They hugged one last time and she was gone. Ailia watched her go before turning back to Kiana.

"You need to let him in." Kiana told her.

"Why should I? All that he has done is make more work for me. He let the roosters in the hen house, for crying out loud," Ailia told her as she slumped to a stool exasperated.

"He has never been a farm hand before. Mistakes happen, that is what makes life an adventure. Give him a second chance. He might learn from you yet."

Ailia sighed and stood. "I'll think about it, but I won't make any promises. I have to get going, Kiana. There is so much work to be done yet."

Ailia put on her shall and walked out of the house and mounted Solas just as the first bolt of lightning struck a tree deep in the forest.

Chapter Six

The storm rolled in just as Ailia got back to the farm. Aiden waved her over and she galloped to the barn to meet him trying to stay dry. She jumped off Solas and led her into her stall. He showed her the reeds and grass that he collected. He had thought it wise to bring them in for the night with the storm. Ailia looked the crates over and was happy with his harvest, though she kept that thought to herself. She bid him a good night and headed to the house to get out of the rain.

Once inside, she discovered her mother slumped in a kitchen chair passed out. Ailia moved the half-empty spirit bottle to the counter and cleaned up the mess of food left on the table. She picked up her mother and carried her to bed, tucking her in before retiring to her own bed to sleep through the raging storm.

The storm had mostly cleared by the next morning and Ailia dressed and went about her morning routine. Aiden joined her and helped her feed the animals. Breakfast was a quiet affair and as soon it was over the pair went out to the barn. The first thing that Ailia did was to grab a shovel from the supply room and motioned to Aiden to follow her. She went to the corner of the barn that was unoccupied and she used the tip of the shovel to mark out where she wanted the egg warmer to go.

"Dig a hole where I marked at least a foot deep," Ailia told him. Aiden nodded and grabbed the shovel from her. She took off into the woods. As she walked the forest paths Ailia looked for some large branches that had fallen during the storm. When she had found a dozen or so that would make suitable logs she headed back to the farm. When she arrived Aiden was just finishing up the hole. Ailia set the logs down and looked at his work.

"Good now let's get these new logs split, the first step is going to be a simple box."

Aiden nodded and went to get the ax. He came back to the barn and quickly split the logs into usable pieces. They set out the frame of the box and working on opposite corners they tied the logs together. Then Ailia took some of the grass Aiden had harvested the day before and began to weave the bottom of the box.

As she was weaving she asked Aiden if he could find her half a dozen long twigs and twice as many shorter ones. He nodded and went off searching. After a while, he came back with the materials and Ailia wove them into the reeds and then tied them to the box.

She tested the strength of the box and seemed to be happy with it. Next, she took several shorter logs and drove them halfway into the ground around the perimeter of the hole Aiden had dug.

"Okay now if we have done this correctly that box should rest on these supports."

Aiden grabbed the box and sure enough, it rested nicely on the supports.

"So how is this box supposed to work?" He asked.

"It's been about five years since I made one but the next step is to line the box with some rough cloth and that's what we will lay the eggs in. Each one has to be turned a couple of times a day so we will have to mark the eggs. Then in the hole you dug we will make a cool burning fire. Last time I used wet leaves that smoldered more than caught fire. The goal is to keep the eggs warm but not overly hot otherwise they will end up cooking. The whole set up is meant to mimic a hen's nest."

"How long do you have to keep this up?"

"Three to four weeks. Now once you get used to it this will be your job since you let the roosters in the hen house."

Aiden nodded and rubbed his neck. He turned to her and then asked, "When will we start collecting eggs?"

"A few days from now. We won't start the warming until we have collected all the eggs we think are fertilized."

"Why is that?"

Ailia looks at him and rolls her eyes before answering, "So they will all hatch at the same time."

"Is that all we have to worry about?"

"I wish it were that easy but no. Once we begin to warm them we will need to weed out the ones not growing."

"How are we supposed to do that when they are still in the shell?"

"It's very complicated," Ailia paused and laughed, "Actually it really isn't. You hold the egg up to a light source and see if you can see the chick developing."

Aiden laughed as well and asked, "Is that all with the chickens?"

Ailia nodded briefly and then said, "Since we are pretty much set up for the eggs now let's get to the rest of the reeds, they need to be woven together. We need them to make a roof for the structure we started a few days ago."

The pair worked the rest of the day on the roof of the wagon cover stopping only to eat lunch and supper. By the time the first stars were starting to twinkle the structure had taken on an almost finished look. Ailia stood back and took stock of their work.

she thought. She bid Aiden a good night and headed into the house. She doused the main fire and then headed to bed.

Much to her relief, the night passed without dreams and she awoke the next morning to a deep grey sky and the start of another rain storm. Ailia worried that there wouldn't be enough time to wax the roof of the new building before the rainy season hit the farm in full force. Since little could be done outside, Ailia left Aiden to feed all of the animals. While the rain came down in sheets outside Ailia spent the morning prepping the berries and other vegetables for canning. After Aiden had finished feeding the animals he joined her in the kitchen dripping wet. He walked over to the hearth and tried to warm his hands but the fire was barely burning.

He turned to Ailia and asked, "Do you mind if I build up the fire a bit."

Ailia bit her lip for a second and then said, "I suppose but if you do it's your responsibility."

"Do you not like fire?" He asked as he grabbed a few logs and fed them into the maw of the fire.

"I don't mind it most of the time but I do respect that it can be very dangerous so I do try to avoid it unless it is needed."

"I can understand that and you're right, it is very dangerous in the wrong hands," Aiden said as he pulled off his overshirt and hung it by the fire to dry.

At that moment Ailia noticed he was still wearing the same clothes that he came into town wearing over a week ago now. She thought about it for a moment and realized that she had never seen him wear anything else and she asked him, "Do you own any other clothes?"

"No, I used to, I guess, but I have had to pack light lately, with all of the moving around. I've gradually lost things along the way."

Ailia disappeared into the back for a few minutes. When she returned she held a couple sets of work clothes and handed them to Aiden.

"These used to be my father's but you're welcome to them he doesn't use them now that he's not in the fields. They are sturdy work clothes and they should serve you well," she paused and looked at him standing there soaked to the bone. She pointed down the hall and continued speaking, "If you want to change your welcome to my bedroom for a minute."

"Thank you," Aiden said blushing and he started to walk to her room.

"Don't. Thank me that is. I'm not doing this because I care one iota about you. I just don't need a sick farm hand hanging about. Now change. Even though it's raining there is still work to be done." Ailia told him and then turned back to preparing her ingredients. Aiden was back quickly and after hanging his clothes to dry he walked over next to Ailia and asked what he could do to help. Ailia directed him to take the prepared food and put it into the jars. He did so and slowly they filled the kitchen table with jars of vegetables. The fruits were all put in a heavy pot and Ailia added some sugar from the market to it. Aiden then carried the pot to the hearth and nestled it in coals so that it could boil and thicken into jam.

While the fruit bubbled and boiled away Ailia took a second pot and started to add spices and salt. When all of the ingredients had been added Ailia sent Aiden out for water. He filled the pot almost full and then also set it by the fire to boil. At her direction, he set this pot closer to the flames and it boiled quickly. Once it had been cooked enough Ailia, with Aiden's help, poured the pickling liquid over the vegetables in all of the jars. They then sealed the jars and box by box took them down to the cellar to cure.

As Aiden took the last box down, Ailia went outside to look at the sky. She stood just off the porch in the rain and looked up taking a moment to clear her mind. As she thought about the last week the rain poured down on her.

, Ailia thought and closed her eyes,

"You'll catch a cold, come in from the rain," Aiden called from the porch. Ailia ignored him and continued to let the raindrops fall on her upturned face.

Ailia thought as she stood there. Her thoughts trailed off and the rain started to come down harder. Aiden watched her from the porch trying to decide what to do. When he could no longer stand to watch her get soaked to the bone, he ran out and tried to pull her from her thoughts by grabbing her shoulder.

The action startled Ailia and she fought back against him. As he grabbed her shoulder she swung at him and he ducked out of the way. He called out her name but she didn't seem to hear him. He backed off for a second but as the rain came down harder he tried to grab her hand. She eluded his grasp but lost her footing in the mud and slipped. Landing in a muddy puddle shocked Ailia and she gasped. She looked up and saw Aiden standing there.

"What are you playing at? Attacking me?" She screamed at him and she pulled herself to her feet ignoring the hand that Aiden held out for her.

"I didn't attack you. I tried to pull you from the rain."

"I don't believe you. From the moment I met you all you have done is go behind my back and make my life more complicated. All you want to do is hurt me."

"I went behind your back only because I needed the job. If you had listened to me or did anything other than blow me off completely, I wouldn't have had to." He shouted at her over the rain.

"You could have moved on to the next town and found a job there. I was an intentional choice and I want to know why." She shouted back at him.

"ENOUGH," Waylin yelled at the pair from the porch.

Ailia shrunk away from Aiden and turned to her father. She bowed her head and mumbled something to her father as she walked into the house. Waylin paid no mind to Aiden and walked in behind her. Left out in the rain, he stared at the front door for a few moments before the yelling started. Even with the roar of the sky, he could hear Waylin calling Ailia several names that he wouldn't even call an enemy. His blood boiled at this.

, Aiden thought and he almost went up to the house. He stopped at the front door and remembered his mission. He turned and stomped into the barn. He climbed up into the loft and tried to fall asleep.

Chapter Seven

Ailia woke when the sun flooded into her room. She could still feel that her face was quite puffy and she could still see the handprints from where Waylin grabbed her arms last night. She rubbed her neck and stretched her back wincing. She turned and saw the tip of a large bruise that had formed on her back where she had been thrown against the wall as her father yelled at her for being irresponsible among other things. She put on a long sleeve shirt to cover them and finished dressing slowly, not wanting to face the world. When she made it out into the kitchen, she splashed her face with some cool water.

She took a deep breath and turned to leave the house. That is when she saw the basket full of eggs. She shook her head and went outside. She noticed that the hens were happily clucking as they scratched at their food scraps.

She went into the barn and saw the horses' food had been topped off and their water filled. She climbed up into the loft to find Aiden but he wasn't there. She shook her head again and climbed down.

She headed out to the field to see if the storm had done any damage. That is where she saw Aiden. He was removing broken stalks and weeds as he went down the rows of vegetables. Ailia didn't know what to say so instead she left him to it and went to the wagon house instead. She inspected it and noticed that there was a little bit of damage from the storm. She quickly fixed the few holes and then went back to the field.

"I'm headed to town to get the wax for the wagon shed I'll be back soon," Ailia told Aiden.

He nodded and kept working not knowing what else to say. A few minutes later he saw her ride down the path on Solas. He finished weeding and then worked on harvesting the little remaining vegetables. He stored them in the wagon. As he was finishing what he thought to be the last harvest of the year, Ailia rode up on her mare, Solas. She jumped down and inspected his work.

"I see you were busy while I was gone," She remarked and he nodded.

"What needs to be done with the wax?" Aiden asked.

"Well let's get it melted first and then we will need to brush it on to the roof," Ailia explained and then directed Aiden to grab the wax from Solas' saddle bags and begin to melt it over a low heat.

Aiden did as he was told and as the wax melted, he folded the clothing he had left to dry the night before and quickly ran them up to the barn loft. He came back, stirred the wax and then carried the pot of melted wax out to Ailia. She had taken the roof panels off the structure and together they worked quickly to make sure they could coat both sides of the roof. With the remaining wax, they were able to do a coat on the outside walls of the wagon shed as well. Once the wax cooled and hardened the pair worked together to permanently attach the roof.

"Now if you will pour the remaining wax into one of the small baskets in the supply room we will save it for any other repairs we might need. Then we need to split the rest of the logs from the other day and build a box for the eventual chicks."

Aiden grabbed the pot of wax and followed Ailia into the barn. They spent the rest of the afternoon and into the night working on the warming box for the new chicks. when they parted ways both were exhausted. Aiden quickly fell into a deep slumber in the loft whereas Ailia looked out her window up into the night sky. After the previous evening, her thoughts were turbulent. She passed much of the night time pondering many things before finally getting a bit of shut-eye near dawn.

The next few days passed quickly. Ailia made a few trips to town to sell the remaining of the unfertilized eggs and the last of her harvest as well. The whole while Aiden stayed working on the farm. He tended to the animals and had even begun to be a familiar face with the horses. They never talked about the night in the rain. Ailia was careful not to show him the bruises, but she had decided that she would let Aiden in at least as much as she was able. She only let him in a little bit here and there. A week after the rooster mix up finally came and Aiden collected the eggs and put them to store in the warming box. Ailia marked each egg on one side with a bit of charcoal.

The mornings dealt with the eggs and the afternoons consisted of canning and readying the farm for the massive amount of rain they would be getting in the coming months. Ailia had Aiden save several of each of the vegetables for seeds before tilling the field. They pruned back the berry bushes and by the end of the week they had all the eggs collected and were just about ready to start the warmer. They took one day to gather damp leaves that were plentiful in the woods around the farm.

Ailia removed the warming box from the posts and gently set it on the ground next to the hole. She put several logs in the hole they had dug and lit them on fire. Aiden slowly shoveled the damp leaves on the logs to create a gentle smolder. Once the smolder was at a good level they moved the box back to the posts and made sure the charcoal mark was facing up on all of them.

"So now keep that at the same temperature for the next twenty one days and with any luck, we should have chicks by then. Oh and the eggs should be turned at least twice a day. "

"Got it. You can trust me. I won't let you down." Aiden told her.

Ailia looked into his eyes and for a moment she was sure that he wasn't talking about the eggs. She turned away as the warmth came to her cheeks. She made her way inside and down into the cellar leaving him to watch over the eggs. Once down in the cellar she checked on the first batch of canning by opening a jar up and tasting some of her pickled vegetables. They were delicious and crunchy.

thought and started to carry up the crates of jars. It took her a few trips to carry the crates up the stairs to pile on the front porch. Once they were all up on the porch she took them to the wagon and then told Aiden that she would be heading to town to sell the first batch of canning.

The next week brought the start of the rainy season and it did just that. As they settled in for the season, Aiden was diligent with the eggs and some days Ailia only saw him for a meal a day or if she took a run to the barn to visit the horses. She spent most of her days repairing clothes for the family, weaving baskets and tending to preserved food in the cellar, all the things she only had time for in the rain.

Aiden loved watching the rain as he meditated and watched the eggs. After the first week, he began to check each of the eggs for a growing chick by holding a candle to them. He separated out those that were not growing and took them to the compost. This process continued on until Aiden awoke one morning to the sound of faint tapping coming from the box. He went and got Ailia who was already up and baking bread. She wiped her hands on her apron and walked out to the barn with him.

"The chicks are almost here," she said, with a grin on her face.

"That's what I thought that tapping meant."

"When the first one pops out, come and get me, okay?"

He nodded and Ailia turned and headed back into the house to tend to the bread. It wasn't long before Aiden was coming up to the porch to grab Ailia away again. They watched as one by one little yellow chicks popped out of their shells.

"Should we start moving them to the larger box?" Aiden asked.

"No not yet wait until they are all hatched. Then you can move them over."

Aiden nodded and continued to watch the chicks as Ailia slipped away back into the kitchen. It took most of the day and into the night before all the baby chickens had tapped through their shells. He watched and then began to gently move them into the insulated nesting box. All told they had fifty-eight chickens' hatch. Ailia was impressed with Aiden's diligence and was even happier when the first of the town folks showed up in spite of the rain to purchase their new roosters and hens. All told they managed to sell fifty of the new hatches.

After the chickens were gone, the rainy season seemed to drag on for longer than normal. It was only made worse by the fact the loft of the barn had become unlivable. A nasty storm had catapulted a tree branch right through the roof and after that Waylin saw fit to have Aiden bunk in the living room of the small farmhouse. Thus the rainy season passed in cramped quarters and gloomy moods.

Chapter 8

As the rainy season began to draw to an end, Ailia's mood changed. She became excited about simple things like planning the layout of the farm and counting down the days until the ground was finally dried out enough that they could begin to cultivate the earth. During the storms, Ailia had made another eight bushels and was eager to have them filled. She also couldn't wait to kick Aiden back into the loft the moment she was sure it wouldn't rain eighty percent of the time.

Though she was still frustrated with him being there she actually had grown used to having a second hand around. She just didn't want him in such close proximity. It was a slow change but as earth dried they worked on repairing the roof. It was up to par just as the last of the puddles had soaked back into the ground. They spent a week laying out the rows of vegetables and planting the seeds from last season. It took another two weeks for them to sprout and the morning after Ailia was happy with their growth she made an announcement at breakfast.

"Well, we are down to a quarter of a crate of meat. So I'm going on a hunting trip and I'll be gone for three days. I'm sure that the three of you can manage without me for that long at least."

Everyone looked stunned for a moment and Ailia almost thought she'd get away with it but then Waylin put down the nail he had been trying to straighten and looked at her with a scowl on his face. "When will you ever learn you, insolent, incompent excuse for a human. You do not get to tell me what you will be doing. I am the one in charge here. How dare you try to tell me what you will be doing. Your mother and I can handle the farm for three days. I didn't hire Aiden to do that, I hired him to make sure you don't mess up. That includes hunting trips."

"I've been going hunting alone for years. I don't need a babysitter."

"You insolent child. You could not even keep a rooster from a chicken. How do you expect me to trust you to go hunting on your own?"

Ailia slammed her hand down on the table and yelled, "I don't need him."

Aiden stayed silent as Waylin stood getting red in the face and through clenched teeth he hissed, "I don't care what you need. You're taking Aiden and there will be no more discussion."

Ailia opened her mouth but her father growled at her and raised his hand. She shut it again. Waylin nodded gruffly and left the table heading out towards his workshop and Rhona followed without a word, leaving Ailia glaring at Aiden sitting across the table from her.

"We are leaving in ten minutes," Ailia muttered as she walked out of the kitchen and into her bedroom. She stripped out of her work clothes and into a pair of thick deer-skin leather pants and long sleeve knit top and over that she tied her stiff padded braces to her forearms. Ailia slung her quiver and bow across her back and headed outside stopping only for a moment by her bedroom door to grab her knapsack.

Aiden stood outside, waiting, and leaning against the side of the barn. A cocky half grin crept across as she strode towards him and he remarked, "You look good in leather."

Ailia rolled her eyes and spat at him, remembering her dislike of him. "Shove it. Now follow me and do try to keep up. I'm not responsible if you get lost."

Ailia took off in a sprint into the woods and didn't pause to see if Aiden was following.

, she thought as she traveled deep into the woods in search of a deer. It was late in the day and the sun was well past midpoint before Ailia spotted fresh tracks. She knelt down and tried to get the scent of the animal. When she had it, she turned and looked behind her to see if Aiden was there. He was and she motioned for him to stay quiet as she led them along the deer's path. A short while later they came to a clearing that Ailia immediately recognized as the one from her dream she had the morning Aiden came into her life. Just like in her dream the buck was panting as he lowered his head to drink from the stream the wound through the pasture.

Ailia motioned for Aiden to stay and silently climbed the nearest tree. She drew her bow out of her quiver and loaded it. She aimed, steadied herself and released the arrow. It flew with a whistle and struck the deer in the rib cage. As the wounded animal fled Ailia jumped from the tree and chased after her prey without a second thought. It took some time for the deer to lose enough blood and collapse, giving up and laying down to die further up the stream. She knelt by the deer, grabbed her knife from her ankle and slit the deer's throat clean through the vein and felt the warm blood pulse over her hand. As the blood trickled from the expiring deer Ailia heard a twig snap and her head jerked up and looked around the area. She spotted Aiden standing several feet away.

"Have you ever seen a deer die this way?" Ailia asked him.

"Don't worry about me, I've seen my fair share of death." He responded curtly as he took several steps closer. "Would you like some help?"

Ailia pointed to her pack. "There's a rope in there, let's tie him to a truss and raise him into a tree before we bed down for the night. It's getting too dark to go home tonight."

Aiden grabbed the rope from her open pack and tied the deer's front and back hooves together. As he did, he asked Ailia, "Are you always lucky enough to find your prey on your first day hunting?"

"No, I don't always, but sometimes, apparently." Ailia paused and was tempted to mention her dream but decided against it.

Aiden remarked it 'must be me.'

She laughed dryly and shook her head as she walked to the stream. She knelt to clean off the blood from her hands and blade. Aiden finished tying both the animal's front and back legs as Ailia grabbed a nearby branch and tied a second of rope to the center of it and threw the rope over a tree branch high off the ground. She tied the deer's legs to either side of the branch and with Aiden's help they hoisted the buck up off the ground and into the air away from predators for the night.

"Well, it's getting dark so we might as well make camp."

Aiden nodded and said, "What would you like me to do?"

"Start the fire please." She responded before disappearing into the woods.

Aiden sighed and gathered bits of kindling into a pile. He looked around to make sure Ailia had left. When he was sure she had gone he looked at the pile of kindling and with a flick of his finger a single flame appeared. With that flame, Aiden started the fire simply by dropping it onto the pile. Ailia returned mere moments later with a small arm full of fallen branches and set them by the fire. She unrolled her blanket and sat cross-legged on it.

"You can do Magick... I saw you."

Aiden smiled his cocky half smile. "Are you sure about that?"

"Don't you go telling me I'm crazy too? My Parents already say that enough."

"What do they say?"

"Only those who are insane claim to have Magick. Kiana disagrees. I've never seen Magick before so I don't know which to believe."

"What do you want to believe 'Lia? Aiden asked, stirring the fire with a long stick.

"Don't call me 'Lia."

"Sorry, Ailia," He paused. "What do you want to believe?" He asked again.

"I don't know. I'd love to believe Kiana and the stories she told when I was growing up but I've never seen Magick. At least not until just now. I mean if that's what I did see." Ailia muttered looking at the ground and pulled her knees to her chest.

Aiden paused for a second thinking. "They are wrong you know."

Ailia looked at him and his left hand burst into a dancing flame.

"It is real. All of it, every story is real." Ailia whispered, her eyes glued to the flame in his hand.

"Yes, the stories are true."

Aiden entertained them with several dancing flames as more stars began to shine in the night sky.

"So who taught you to hunt?" He asked as the fire danced against the darkness of the night.

"It was the same person who taught me to farm, and about the animals."

"And who was that?" Aiden asked again.

"Well, it wasn't my mother or my father. I learned most of what I know from the animals and the plants. Kiana taught me a few things here and there where she could. I don't know if you noticed but I have had to be rather self-sufficient," Ailia answered as she watched the fire with a new appreciation.

She pondered a question for a moment and then finally asked, "How long have you known you were a fire mage?"

"The first time I was able to control fire was when I was seven years old I think."

"What was it like?

"Really scary, I was in primary school. It was the year before we had to pick if we wanted to go into the military training school or the civic works academy. We were in class learning about the different elements and one of my classmates thought it would be funny to knock over the lantern of fire when the teacher had their back turned. No one stopped the kid because they didn't think anything else would catch on fire since the lantern was on a stone counter. We were wrong and quickly became trapped behind a wall of fire that spread from one side of the room to the other and blocked all of us from the door.

"As the fire and smoke grew we huddled against the back wall. All I can remember thinking is that I didn't want anyone else to die this way so I broke from the huddle and attempted to jump through the flames. I had hoped to be able to run for help but as I jumped, I realized the flames were not hot. I landed in the middle of the fire and stood there for a second watching the flames around me. That is when the strangest thing happened. I could hear the flame speak to me. I told it to stop burning everything and that if it stopped and came with me that I would find something that it could burn. The flame agreed and in an instant, it flickered once and shrank until it all but vanished into several puffs of smoke. The little flame that was left sat cozily in my hand. The teacher ushered me out of the room and to the kitchen where I was able to give the flame a purpose."

Ailia sat there mesmerized for a couple minutes after he was done with his story and then finally asked, "Military Training School? Where did you grow up? What happened after that?"

"I grew up with the Cosantóirí. They have a headquarters not known to anyone who isn't a member. I was born and raised there. As for what happened to me next, nothing special really, I mean I had to go to the training grounds a couple of days after classes each week. Well, that and my parents sat me down and had a talk with me about my use of fire. Apparently, my mother thought I would start throwing fireballs at people now that I could. Truth be told it was years before I was comfortable with doing anything with my powers. Outside the training grounds, I wouldn't even light a fire with

Magick. You were right a while back when you said that fire is a dangerous thing."

"So you really are a member? What brings you all the way out here?"

"Honestly I needed a change. I fully believe in the cause but camp politics can be a bit much. And you? Are you a member as well?"

"I have always been reserved in my judgement. My parents sympathize with the Thren if not outright support them but many of the villagers are victims of Thren violence and that is not something I can condone. I try to stay out of politics as well. All I want is to run my farm without interference from anyone. Be my own person without my parents around to control me."

A silence washed over them for a while as the fire danced against the darkness of the camp. Ailia watched the flames move trying to absorb this new information she was learning about Aiden. Questions swam in her brain and finally she asked, "what kinds of things are you able to do as a fire mage, I mean besides the obvious things like making fire."

"Well, I can heat all sorts of substances, like water, or .....
chicken eggs."

"You didn't," Ailia burst out with a chuckle.

"Yeah, I did. I used Magick to incubate the eggs."

"No wonder we had so many hatchlings. It was near double
what I have been able to get in the past. Is there anything else you
can do?"

"Well, I can also manipulate smoke and steam since they are
superheated air," he said and then had the smoke coming from the
fire form a mirror image of Ailia's face. She looked at the smoke
double of her and couldn't think of anything else to say. Aiden held
the image for a few seconds and then let it drift off into the sky.
They lapsed into silence for a while just watching the fire and smoke
in the quiet night.

Finally, Aiden asked, "What was it like growing up for you?"

"I don't know if I'm ready to share my past. It's not
something I like to talk about."

"I understand," he paused, "You don't deserve how they treat
you."

"It wasn't always this bad you know. I can remember when mammon wasn't drunk all the time. Dad was always a little harsh but mammon used to care more. She used to stand up to him. I didn't know anything but the farm until I was seven. I only left the farm at that point because the village elders kept coming to the homestead to see why I wasn't in school. They worried about my well being I guess or that's what they said. I didn't really care why they were there. I just knew Pa hated it and I wanted to learn so much. I was finally allowed to go for about three years before Mamm took to the spirits. It was during those years that I met Cara and her caretaker and village elder Kiana. Once Mamm was taken by the drink, I didn't have a choice but to start to take care of the farm.

"Pa never did have much of a green thumb but we scraped by. Then when I started working the field the harvests started to get bigger each year. So they withdrew from the farm more and more and left me to it. All they demanded was perfection and spirits."

Not sure what to say to that he let the conversation die out and soon Ailia laid her head down on her knapsack and drifted off to sleep. He watched the fire die slowly as she slept. When his eyes were finally heavy he put the fire out with a flick of his wrist and

also slept.

Chapter Nine

The sun climbed from the horizon and lit the sky with soft

oranges, pale blues and pinks. Its light woke Ailia. She quickly

packed and then nudged Aiden awake as well. The pair quickly

smudged out the traces of their camp and using two long branches

created a rack of sorts to carry the deer home on. The animal slowed

them considerably as they trekked back through the heavy

underbrush. The sun blazed high in the sky above the farm when

they finally came through the tree line. They walked over to the

barn. Ailia pointed out two hooks sticking out from the side of the

barn that Aiden hadn't noticed before. They were almost six feet

apart and the rack they had made for the deer fit them perfectly.

"I'm going to let them know I am back before we skin the

dear and set it to cure. Can you check on the animals?" Ailia asked

as she walked up to the front porch. Aiden nodded and went about

his chores. She walked into the house and the fire in the living room

was barely smoldering. She found it slightly odd but shrugged it off

and went back to her room. She dropped off her knapsack and then

went to her parent's door and knocked. There was no response so

she pushed the slightly ajar door open.

Waylin was in bed with a hot water skin on his head and a dressing holding his arm in a sling. He appeared to be sleeping and next to him on the floor was Rhona curled in a ball hugging an empty jug. She was rocking back and forth as her eyes darted to and fro. Ailia rushed to his side and gently nudged his uninjured shoulder to wake him.

"What happened?"

"Some weird creature bit me yesterday when I was out in the field." He said gruffly before a fit of coughs racked him.

"Has the healer been here?"

"Yeah, he was out here this morning. Not that he ever did us much good. He said I should live as long as the wound is kept clean. He's worried about her more than me." He said and pointed to the near-catatonic Rhona next to him.

Ailia nodded and went over to the other side of the bed. She helped Rhona get up and took her to the kitchen. She guided her to a chair and then went and got a warm washcloth. She washed her face and slowly it seemed that the rocking stopped. Rhona looked out the window and sat still as a statue for a while until Aiden came in from his chores.

"What is going on?" He asked and looked at Rhona. Her gaze shifted from the window to the table.

"Some sort of creature bit Pa yesterday right after we left and he is in pretty rough shape. She isn't handling the situation well."

"I can see that. When was the last time she wasn't on the drink?"

"Try when I was about eight years old," Ailia said and rolled her eyes. She kept running around the house, cleaning up after Rhona's mess just to keep busy.

Aiden watched her for a minute and then said, "That's not good. What can I do to help?"

Ailia pulled out some gems from her pouch and told Aiden to go to the market and pick up more bandages and several jugs of clear spirits to use an antiseptic. She quickly wrote a list of herbs and handed it to him. He nodded and took off. Ailia continued to try and get her mother to snap out of her state. It took a while but finally, it seemed that she might be able to cope now that Ailia was home. About the time Aiden returned with supplies, Rhona had gotten up from the table and started to tend to the fire.

The next several days were long ones. During the first day in between bandage changes, the dear was skinned and portioned out into several cuts from small chunks of meat for soup and some long thin strips of meat for jerky. All of these cuts were then packed in salt and several other seasonings and left to cure in the cellar.

Often during that first night, as her Pa struggled to heal, Ailia was woken by shouts coming from the other room. She wasn't sure what creature had bitten Waylin but it seemed to have some sort of toxin in its saliva. As the toxin worked through his system it slowly stole movement from his toes up. As his legs quit working the toxin also plagued him with disturbing visions and delirious rants about different things. Sometimes it was about different towns folks who had slighted him and other times it was what just what Ailia would consider gibberish. During the second day as Ailia was changing his bandages, he became extremely agitated and with his remaining strength began to thrash his arms about. Ailia called Aiden to help her.

"He was betrayed, BETRAYED I tell you," Waylin said and looked at Ailia unable to focus on her.

"Okay, Pa," she said and patted his good shoulder.

"A good man… left to perish by his brothers….…." Waylin muttered as Ailia put the first of the clean bandages as Aiden held him still.

"Who is this good man," Aiden asked as he handed another strip of bandages to Ailia.

Waylin just kept repeating "one of three" over and over as they worked to finish the bandage and he drifted into an uneasy sleep.

They left him to sleep and walked out of the room, shutting the door behind them.

"Do you know what he was talking about?" Aiden asked as they walked into the kitchen.

Ailia said, "Not a clue, but I am worried about him. I have never seen him like this before. I wish I knew what bit him."

She turned to her chores on the farm and so did Aiden. She went out to the crops and worked on weeding them and making sure that they were progressing correctly. She also helped them along with some generous scoops of the compost heap. It was Aiden's job to corral a few chickens that had stopped laying eggs. When he had the four hens caught he placed them in the old warming box the chicks had stayed in months earlier. He kept them there until Ailia had finished with the fields. She joined him and together they butchered the chickens.

It was then to the next steps including draining the blood and a quick blanch. This made it so the feathers could be more easily plucked. Those feathers were destined for a pillow or new mattress as soon as they could be taken from the chicken. Taking the feathers off took them nearly the whole afternoon. It only took longer because every time they got into a rhythm someone from the house called for them. When the feathers were finally off the chickens and stored in a basket for later use, Ailia took two of them and shoved them into the salt cure with the deer meat. The others she put on to boil to create a lovely broth, hoping it would help Waylin heal.

Waylin continued to have a high fever for a few days and the bite marks on his arm refused to scab over. As his condition worsened Rhona slipped back into her stupor. His rants became more violent and with each one Rhona withdrew inside herself to shut them out.

"Kill... Kill those who betrayed.... Kill all who have...." He muttered one time as Ailia tried to spoon feed him some of the chicken broth. He was still muttering when she left the room but she forced herself to pay no attention. A while later Aiden went in and also tried to get him to eat some of the broth.

"Who do you want to kill," Aiden asked. Waylin muttered "Magick" and then he strung together the name that Aiden had begun to dread, Drecan Undergallows.

he thought to himself,

Aiden continued to try and feed Waylin as he pondered his next steps. When he got up and turned to leave Waylin gasped and his eyes grew wide. Aiden quickly tried to cover the garnet stones of his dagger hilt but it was too late, they had been seen.

"I know who you are, Aiden. I know why you have come, but your hope is lost. She has no connections with anything or anyone. She cannot access what you think she can." He whispered so only he could hear.

"She will know how the Cosantóirí murdered her parents and that we took her in. That's what I'll tell her, you see, next time she comes to tend to me."

In a split second Aiden's arms locked around the weakened man's neck. As he held him there Aiden whispered, "You will not have a chance to lie to her anymore."

Waylin laughed as if he knew something else but quickly passed out in the hold. Aiden released him and tucked in the now passed out Waylin. He left the room quickly and told Ailia that he had passed out.

"I'm going to go fetch Kiana maybe in her wisdom she will have the answers we need."

Ailia nodded and Aiden ran from the house. He sprinted through the woods as quick as he could and arrived at Kiana's back door winded. Before he had a chance to knock ,however, it opened.

"What brings you here on this rather cloudy morning?"

"Waylin… knows," Aiden panted out.

Kiana ushered him inside for a moment and gave him something to drink. Aiden took a sip of water and then urgently told Kiana what had happened since they returned back from their hunting trip. By the time he was done talking his breathing had returned to normal.

"This is grave indeed," Kiana responded and then started to rifle through her kitchen cupboards. She grabbed several bunches of herbs and slipped them into a pouch before turning back to Aiden.

"Is he subdued for now?"

"Aye, I put him in a physically induced slumber and then came right here as fast as my feet would take me."

"Good."

The pair left and took a shortcut through the woods, arriving at the farm less than an hour after Aiden had left.

Ailia was relieved to see Kiana and gave her a quick hug.

"Child, where is he? Let me see what I can do." Kiana said after the hug as she rolled up her sleeves. Ailia led her to the bedroom and Kiana looked over Waylin.

"Here help me undo the bandage I want to see the bite marks." Ailia helped her unwind the bandage and expose the festering wounds.

"I have tried everything from using spirits to cleanse the wounds and a hot slave made like you showed me the one time the thorns on the prickle briar scraped my leg so bad."

"You have done well my child but these wounds are far from any prickle briar. I think that these bite marks are caused by a very nasty creature. They are four-legged small creatures with very sharp front teeth. Those teeth are coated with a progressive toxin that slowly paralyzes the victim. These creatures typically only live in the far northern provinces of Mynor. They are called nimh. I wasn't aware they had ever ventured or could even survive this far south. I have some herbs from home with me that might help. Can you go boil some water for me?" Ailia nodded and left the room, closing the door behind her.

Chapter Ten

Kiana stood at the foot of the bed and grabbed her satchel of herbs and picked one leaf out that would awaken the slumbering man in front of her. Waving it under his nose he jerked at the smell and his eyes flashed open.

"You too, Kiana? Can we trust no one these days?" Waylin muttered.

"Yes, me too. We are closer than you think. I know what you have done and who Ailia really is. Make no mistake you will not succeed while there is still air in my lungs. You may think that you broke that precious little girl a long time ago with what you have done but I assure you that you are wrong. You're not the only force in her life. Now tell me what you know and I'll make your death quick."

"I will never tell you anything." He strengthened himself against her gaze.

She grabbed his wound, dug a finger into it and looked at him with her icy gaze and said. "You will die no matter what. There is no hope but that I can stop your suffering."

His strength and resolve had been broken by the toxins in his body and he took only one moment to think. Kiana released her grip and listened closely, "She was a job. We were supposed to kill her after it was done, but Rhona fell in love with her pretty green eyes and her laughter. I love Rhona, regardless of what else I'm guilty of. The worst thing I ever did was bring her into my work. Because of it, we couldn't have our own children, so I let her keep the babe…." Waylin trailed off into another rant unable to form whole words. Kiana passed the same leaf under his nose again and it seemed to bring his mind back from the edge.

"For the first few years, we continued on missions. Drecan was furious when he found out we had kept her, kept your hope alive. But after he met her, he couldn't bear the order any longer. His new plan was darker though, worse than death almost. We settled here and our job was to break her soul so she could never wield her powers against him. He was afraid of her or at least a part of him was. We tried our best but I guess we failed…."

Kiana quickly grabbed the herbs she needed to finish off Waylin, her anger boiling over. As she went to apply them to the festering wounds, he asked her to wait.

"I'm not quite finished," he paused, struggling to stay present, "I remember he said something when he met her. It struck me as a bit odd at the time but since you seem to be aware of the workings in Mynor maybe it will make sense to you."

"Go on," Kiana urged him.

"He said 'My family, you know, they think me dead. Maybe one day they will think her dead as well and their hope will die with her. Maybe that is my true revenge.'"

Upon hearing that Kiana's eyes watered slightly. Without another thought applied the herbs. Moments later Ailia came through the door with boiling water, when she did Waylin quickly shut his eyes and pretended to still slumber making peace with what was to come. Together they soaked the bandages in the water and then applied them to the wounds.

"He needs rest now, child and I must warn you this may not be enough to save him."

"The healer said he'd be alright."

"I doubt the doctor has seen a bite like this before but I shall tell him what to do lest anyone else gets bitten by a nimh."

Ailia felt her skin prickle at Kiana's news and her mood darkened to match the storm clouds that had been rolling in over the past few hours. She nodded and they walked out of the room to let Waylin rest. Thunder and lightning began to rumble in the sky. Rhona seemed to come out of her stupor with the first crack lighting and demanded to see her husband. Kiana tried to soothe the woman and told her that Waylin needed to rest. It was to no avail and she went back to the bedroom. A shrill yell followed and everyone rushed in behind her.

"He's dead," She wailed and then turned and pointed to Kiana, "And you killed him."

"Mammon she did nothing of the sort. She tried to save him from the toxins," Ailia tried to reason with her as the sky opened up and cried with them.

"It's alright Ailia she has every right to accuse me and it is a very difficult thing to lose one's husband," Kiana said, remaining calm though Aiden could see the very real pain in her eyes.

Rhona collapsed down to the floor in her grief. Aiden carried her to the kitchen and sat her in a chair while Kiana fixed her a powerful sleeping draught. Soon the heartbroken woman was asleep on a makeshift cot. As she slept Ailia told Aiden where he could start digging as they needed to prepare Waylin's body for the next life. Kiana helped Ailia bring the body out to the kitchen table on a sheet and they removed the bandages.

Ailia put a pot of water on to boil and then left in search of fruit and other spices that were traditionally buried with the dead. As Ailia walked through the woods she couldn't feel the rain even though it stormed around her. Ailia looked up and it was almost as if she had an invisible shield protecting her.

It was a tradition that the child does this alone if able as a way to mourn the passing of a father and to honor his life. As Ailia walked the woods and Aiden dug the grave, Kiana dressed the corpse in clean clothes burning the ones he had worn at the time of passing along with the bandages and anything else that may have touched the toxins. Later that evening when all of the preparations had been made, Rhona was brought from her slumber and they quietly buried Waylin behind the house.

When the last shovel of dirt was placed over his body Kiana bid them a good night and left them to their sadness. For the next two days, Aiden took care of the farm as neither Ailia nor Rhona left their respective bedrooms. On the third day, as Aiden tended to the farm, he could feel Ailia's pent-up energy and he wondered what she was feeling.

she thought on the third day after her father's passing.

. Ailia sighed as her heart screamed at her. She knew that it was custom to wait three days before emerging from her grief-stricken solitude but her tears had dried up the first day after she realized the farm was hers to run with even more freedom than before. The second day she had spent pacing around her room thinking about all the things she wanted to do. Finally on the third day, Ailia decided she could no longer stand the four walls she had been in. Looking out her window to make sure no one was around Ailia jumped from her room and took off in a sprint not caring where she was going just knowing she didn't want to be in that house anymore, even if it was proper to grieve alone.

she thought as she broke free from the gloom that hung about the farm.

As she ran, she thought of everything that had happened in the past few days.

he thought as the soles of her shoes pounded against the ground. Her mind raced and with every stride another thought.

she decided as she reached the bank of a wide river and realized she was quite a ways away from home. Her knees buckled and she knelt at the river's edge. She took several long drinks from the river and then tried to calm the thoughts in her head. Try as she might the thought of Aiden couldn't be held at bay.

The river's languid current gently tumbled stones and other debris downstream, but a young tree branch stuck out of the water. It had been caught between two larger boulders and bobbed up and down in the river. The current caught it ever so often and pulled it forward only to have it spring back when it could go no further.

She stripped off her outer layer of clothes and dove into the river. She freed the branch from the rock. She watched it float away, longing to follow it, but knowing she couldn't. She swam for a while, diving every so often to examine the river bottom. Ailia let her worries wash over her with the current as she swam.

When the sun had passed midpoint, she walked out of the river and laid down in a grassy patch nearby to let her clothes dry.

As she stared at the clouds in the sky, her mind finally calmed enough to allow her some much-needed rest.

The chirping of several birds awoke Ailia several hours later and she put on her outer clothes. The sun sank lower and the cool night air blew around Ailia, chilling her as she made her way back home. It was dark and the stars were sparkling when she got there, but she still looked from the tree line to see if anyone was hanging around the house. She saw no one and ran across the field slipping back into her room. Tomorrow she could emerge from her mourning time and get back to work. As the nightingales broke into song Ailia laid down on her bed and fell asleep planning on what she would do first tomorrow.

Ailia emerged before dawn with puffy eyes. The clouds that had hung heavy over the farm began to float away, leaving the sky clear as the moon faded away and the sun rose. Her skin prickled as she watched the clouds float away.

When the blue sky broke free she went straight to work with the plants. She didn't talk much at first but as the work eased her pain she began to act much as she had before. Rhona, on the other hand, did not recover. She took to spending hours in Waylin's cluttered workshop. When she did emerge she began to rant of his murder by their enemies. She also went nowhere without a bottle of booze in her hand.

A week after Waylin died Ailia and Aiden were working in the field. They were weeding, Aiden on the opposite end of the field from Ailia with his back towards the farmhouse. Rhona ran up behind Aiden out of nowhere and hit him in the back with a full jug of spirits. He stumbled forward and fell to his knees.

"Mammon, what are you doing?" Ailia yelled as she rushed over to them. Aiden quickly got back to his feet rubbing the back of his head.

"I am not your mammon. She is dead, dead with your father," she shouted at Ailia and tried to strike Aiden again, missing her swing wild. Ailia tried to grab at Rhona but Aiden told her to stay back. When her arm extended a third time he was ready for it. He grabbed her wrist and squeezed so she would release the bottle. It fell and with his other hand he caught it and tossed it to Ailia. The loss of her weapon didn't stop Rhona. With her other hand she threw one punch after another aimed at Aiden's jaw. He blocked the punches but had to let go of her wrist to do so. He didn't want to hurt her so he backed away from her when he could. Ailia got closer, wanting to help, but Aiden just told her to stay back again. Eventually she would tire and this would end.

As he continued to evade her, Cedric and Cara rode up in their wagon. He pulled the horses to a stop and then jumped down to help Aiden. With a second person there it took no time to tie up Rhona's hands and get her into the house.

"What was that all about?" Cara asked Ailia, as she waddled over from the wagon.

"She just attacked. It must be out of grief more than anything. At least I hope that is why."

"Kiana came by and told me what happened a few days ago. That's why we are here. Do you need anything?"

"We will make do, but I appreciate it. What about you? Is there anything you need for the baby?"

"Thank you for the offer but I still have plenty of time before the baby arrives," Cara paused and put a hand on Ailia's shoulder, "it's a terrible thing to lose one's father, and it would seem mother as well. It's worse when you know them."

"I don't know if I have lost her yet, but time will tell," Ailia said.

The two walked into the house together. Rhona was still fighting back against Aiden and Cedric but she was getting tired. Her struggles lessened and she finally slumped in the chair Her once pretty brown eyes were puffy and bloodshot. Her hair was unkempt and she was still in the same clothes she wore before Waylin's demise.

"Why did you attack?" Ailia asked her as she sat down across from her.

"It's his fault my husband is dead," she replied tilting her head towards Aiden.

"Aiden didn't kill him, Mammon. The nimh bite did."

"No it was that witch lady, and he is the one that brought her here."

"Kiana was trying to help. It's not her fault it was too late to save him."

"She didn't even try to save him. She's been against us since she tried to take you away from us. Forcing you to go to town school," Rhona spat at Cara and kept ranting, "introducing you to her, a desolate bastard and filling your head with Magickal nonsense. I put an end to that, I did, though. Best thing my drinking ever did. Kept you at home and kept you close......."

Rhona shook her head and began to rock back and forth, but refused to say anything further. The four exited the kitchen to leave her in her grief and walked outside.

Ailia looked at Cara and apologized, "I can't believe she said that. I am so sorry."

"No need to be sorry. I have accepted what I am and so has Cedric. That's all that matters." Cedric wrapped his arm around Cara and pressed a kiss to her forehead before turning back to Ailia.

"What are you going to do with her?" Cedric asked.

"I'm not sure," she replied and then turned to Aiden and asked, "Are you okay?"

"Aye, I'm fine," Aiden said as he rubbed the back of his head, "There was little power behind the blow."

"Do you think she will attack again?"

"She has gone through a lot this last week so only time will tell if she will or not," Ailia said.

"We should let her rest for now."

Everyone stood around for a moment and looked at each other. Not sure what to say next. Finally, Ailia realized that no one had been introduced.

"Aiden, by the way, this is Cara and Cedric. They live out past Latzu, near Kiana."

"Good to meet the both of you. Thank you so much for the help back there Cedric."

"I'm just happy to help." Cedric answered.

"That's why we are here. What can we help with, Ailia?"

Ailia paused for a second and bit her lip. "Honestly, my parents haven't really done anything on the farm since I was pulled out of school. It's not much different now than it was before…," she hesitated and looked at Cara before admitting, "besides I have Aiden now."

"Ailia," Cara looked at her friend and frowned, "I had my suspicions of course but why didn't you tell me? Did you at least tell Kiana?"

"Like I really wanted to admit my Pa was mean and violent or that my Mammon is a drunk. Besides, there was little that you could have helped with. I don't think they even liked the fact that I have one friend. I was shocked when he let Aiden come on as a hand."

"I guess I can understand that but I would have done whatever I could to help."

"I would have as well. So what would you like to do now?" Cedric asked.

"Why don't you guys stay out here. Cara and I will go see if Rhona has calmed down any."

Cedric and Aiden both nodded and started towards the field. Ailia took a deep breath and went back inside with Cara following. She expected to see Rhona hunched over the table or trying to frantically move her arms but she saw none of that. What she did see was a pile of ropes on the floor behind the chair they had put Rhona in.

"She's escaped," Cara whispered as she waddled in behind Ailia.

Ailia said, "I'm going to search the house first."

She went up the hall and checked both bedrooms. Finding nothing she returned to the kitchen.

, "Stay here. Be safe. I want to check the barn as well," she said to Cara as she walked through the kitchen.

The men saw Ailia run from the house and followed her into the barn.

"She escaped, didn't she?" Aiden asked . Ailia nodded and both the men helped her search. It took longer in the barn, checking each of the horses' pens and her father's workshop. Aiden even climbed to the loft to make sure she wasn't hiding up there waiting for him. They found no trace of Rhona so they headed back to the house and called out to Cara. She joined them, as quick as she could waddle out.

"Blast it!"

"Where could she have gone?" Cara asked.

"I'm not sure," Ailia said and hung her head.

"Kiana," Aiden let out a long breath, "I'm sure of it."

Aiden took a breath and let it sink in. Ailia's eyes widened a bit as she realized he had surmised correctly.

"We have to get to her. I would never forgive myself if something happened to Kiana. I'll be fastest on Solas. Aiden you take Iasair. I hope you can ride bareback." Ailia called as she was already halfway back to the barn in a dead-on sprint. Cedric quickly climbed into the wagon and then helped Cara up into the wagon and quickly climbed into the wagon, calling to Ailia that they would meet them there.

Chapter Eleven

Ailia and Aiden rode as fast as the horses would take them, but when they arrived at Kiana's the back door was already banging against the house in the wind and they could hear things falling to the ground from inside. Ailia jumped off of Solas and rushed inside. In the living room, she found Kiana and Rhona wrestling each other. Rhona was screaming 'murderer' at Kiana as she tried to punch her. Kiana grappled back and the pair rolled on the floor. Rhona got away from Kiana and caught her breath for a second before lunging at her and slamming against a bookcase. Several books fell on them as they fought. Neither of them noticed Ailia come into the room as they continued to struggle.

Ailia watched, frozen in horror as the two kept fighting, neither gaining any ground. Aiden came in a few seconds later and jumped in to break up the fight. He pulled Rhona off of Kiana and secured her arms behind her. Kiana stood and straightened her dress. Rhona threw her head back trying to land a blow on Aiden, but his strong arms kept her at bay. Moments later Cedric and Cara joined them and the two men together were able to tie up Rhona.

"You all are cowards and murderers," Rhona spat as they tied her to the chair making sure she wouldn't so easily escape this time.

Kiana looked at her with a steely gaze and said, "The only coward I see here is you," she leaned in closer to her and whispered, "I know everything you did and it didn't work."

Rhona pulled at her bindings and spit at Kiana's face. Once the final knot was tied securing the bindings, the five of them retired to the kitchen and out of earshot of the prisoner.

"Are you hurt Kiana?" Ailia asked.

"No child, I am whole. That was no more than a little excitement."

Ailia let out a deep breath and sat on one of the kitchen stools.

"What are we going to do with her?" Cedric asked.

"She's already attacked Aiden and now you," Cara said, also sitting down.

"She will need to be locked up. Two assaults in one day and one of them on a village elder and witnessed by four citizens. There is no question about it," Kiana said.

"Aye, but why does she think you killed my Pa?" Ailia asked, looking at Kiana.

"Child, anyone would think that in grief. It's probably only because I was there at the time of his passing."

"Do you know what Pa was talking about when he was talking about being betrayed?" She asked.

"There are many things that must now come to the surface. You may not like all that you hear. Secrets are not always pleasant but in this case all are true. First though let us get the criminal far from this place."

Cedric and Aiden went back into the front room undid enough of the rope to allow Rhona to stand, but kept her arms bound as they led her from Kiana's home into town and straight to the sheriff's office. Kiana, Ailia, and Cara followed them closely. It was no surprise to any of them when a crowd began to form at the spectacle. Murmurs ruffled through the crowd as they got closer to the sheriff's office. When they arrived, the Sheriff came outside.

"What is this all about, Kiana?" he demanded.

"This woman attacked Aiden this morning at Ailia's farm and then came this afternoon and attacked me. I want her jailed while the other elders discuss her punishment."

The crowd gasped at the revelation, but the sheriff did as Kiana asked and soon the excitement died down as did the crowd. The five of them made their way back to Kiana's place.

They started by cleaning up the mess made earlier. Ailia picked up books and put them back on the shelf while Cara fixed tea in the kitchen. The men helped Kiana straighten up the knocked over furniture. They soon had the house straightened and were all crammed in the living room with cups of tea in their hands.

Kiana took a sip of her tea, "Ailia you said earlier that the actions of the last few days have left you with more questions than answers. Tell me, child, what are your questions."

"Well, there are so many that I have. I'm not sure which one I want to ask first."

"What is your heart telling you is most important?"

"When Pa was sick he kept ranting about traitors and murders. He said he was betrayed. Do you know what he was talking about?"

"Waylin was talking about the war between Cosantóirí and the Thren, I would suspect. From what I have suspected for a few years now and what I have learned since these events unfolded both Rhona and Waylin are Threnian."

"No" Ailia mouthed.

Aiden reassured her by saying, "Their choices don't have to be yours as well. You can make your own path."

"Aiden is right, my child. Your fate is your own."

Ailia nodded and then asked, "Why did she say she wasn't my Mammon?"

At this Kiana took a deep breath and a long sip of tea before answering, "There are things that you don't yet know about yourself. Things I have only suspected were true until recently. The risk was too great to act without certainty"

"That doesn't answer my question Kiana."

"Do you trust me, child?"

"You have never given me a reason not to trust you."

"There are things that I know that I have not shared. It was done to protect you though you may not see it that way. I will tell you now." Kiana paused, taking a deep breath, "Rhona isn't your Mammon and Waylin wasn't your Pa."

"What are you saying Kiana?" Ailia asked, sucking in a deep breath, her body beginning to shake.

"My child, there is a part of me that hoped I was wrong about what I suspected. I knew this information would completely change your world. Though I always hated your circumstances, I wouldn't do that to you if I wasn't a hundred percent sure. Aiden's arrival proved to me that I was unfortunately right about my suspicions. You were kidnapped when you were still a babe and ordered to be murdered. Everyone feared your demise. I was a part of the original search team. It was pure luck that Waylin and Rhona settled near here. It is obvious now that you were not murdered, and for that I am truly grateful. We may never know why they didn't complete their mission but they didn't."

"Wait a second... What does Aiden have to do with any of this?"

"As you might have guessed he isn't just a traveler. He was sent here to find you by your parents and the Consantóirí High

Council. You're true parents are still out there and they never stopped looking for you."

Ailia looked at Aiden, "This was all a sham. You lied to me. The whole time you worked with me you couldn't say something? Anything? You saw how he was with me and nothing," she trailed off and then turned to Kiana searching for something but not knowing what.

Aiden spoke first, "This wasn't a sham, I promise. Yes, when I arrived here I did know of your true past. I was sent to secure your safety and bring you back to your family but after our first meeting, when I saw the distrust in you, I knew you wouldn't believe me if I just came out with it," Aiden paused steadying his breath, "The work I did on the farm, the stories I told you, and the words I said to you. That is me, that is who I am, all of that is true. I wanted you to trust me before I told you. I thought it would be easier for you."

"Easy," she sputtered out her mouth hanging open before she turned to look Aiden in the eyes, "This couldn't ever be easy." Ailia said and got up. Kiana stood with her and tried to comfort her but she jerked away.

"Ailia, I know you are feeling a lot of emotions right now. I wish things would have played out different but life is not always what we want. I know this is hard but you are not alone, Child. We are all here for you." Kiana told her and tried to comfort her again.

"No. No time and no more lies," Ailia said, shaking her head and then she backed away from the group, leaving the house, and disappearing into the woods. Aiden started after but Kiana stopped him with a hand on his arm.

"Give her some time to process. This is a big change for her."

"Hold on a second," Cara said, "You mean to tell me that Ailia's parents weren't her parents at all. You're saying that they kidnapped her? Whatever became of her real parents?"

"Her real parents, uncle, and family are out there, yes. She is in grave danger now though which is why I held off telling her," Aiden explained.

"Why is she in danger?" Cedric asked.

"Waylin's death and Rhona's attacks have set many things in motion and the Threnian will know that they will no longer be able to use her to aid in their mission. Her alliance to whichever side will tilt the tide of war according to an ancient prophecy. The Threnians will not wait for her to make the choice. They will kill her if they have the chance. We must protect her because even if she doesn't want a part of this war fate is often unkind."

"Back up a second, I thought those battles were long past though. I thought the war was over," Cara said looking at Kiana.

"In this valley, the battles may be in the past but in other parts of the world not so much. The control of the Thren is not as absolute as they would have you believe and there is a resistance growing as whispers and there has been for many seasons. The seeds and thoughts are planted in the conversations of everyday life."

"Ailia is a part of this war then?"

"Yes, she is a very important part of it. Though clearly not by choice."

As Kiana explained things to Cedric and Cara, Aiden slipped out without notice and went to the forest searching for Ailia. His first instinct was to look for a trail but as he suspected she had not left one. Even in her anger, she was invisible in her woods. He took his time going through the forest making sure he didn't miss her in any of the many hiding places. He also took his time to allow her to cool down. As the sun was setting Aiden finally made it back to the farm and there was Ailia working the field. He watched her from the tree line not yet wanting to approach.

As he watched she attacked the weeds with an angry vigor slashing at them and pulling them roughly. She still had a tender touch to her plants. He also noticed the sinking sun didn't seem to bother her at all. By the time he had mustered up the courage to approach it was all but dark and the stars had already begun to peak out of the clear blue sky.

"Ailia," He said softly.

"Go away Aiden," She said, not bothering to look at him or to stop her work.

"I can't do that. Now that you know your history you're in grave danger. There are forces beyond our control that have been set in motion with the events of the last few days."

Ailia finally stood and turned to him, "I don't care about any of that. Knowing what I know changes nothing for me. I am a farm girl and I want to stay a farm girl. So please, I beg you to leave me alone. I will have no part of any of your lies."

Aiden nodded, "I understand that's how you're feeling right now. I will do whatever it takes to protect you and earn back your trust. I am so very sorry."

Without another word and before she could respond, he went off into the woods knowing no other words would reach her right now. He didn't go far but he went just deep enough not to be seen from the farm. He climbed a tree and from there he watched the farm for the rest of the evening. S

, He thought as he kept watch over her,

He remained there until the early morning hours when Kiana emerged on the forest floor next to the tree. He jumped down to the ground and greeted her.

"Did you speak to her last night?"

"Only briefly, she is in pain and being quite stubborn. She wouldn't listen to anything"

"Put yourself in her shoes, my child. She's clinging on to what she knows as the world. Anything that threatens to take that, including those who wish to protect her, takes her from her reality. It can be hard to deal with that amount of change."

"I understand that. I just worry about her and how she will take the other changes that I know must come to pass." He said, his gaze wandering off into the distance.

"This is the biggest shock and once the rest is revealed I think she will do better with the new information."

"I hope so. How much did you tell Cara and Cedric yesterday?"

"They know it all. Well, all but one bit of information. The only bit I spared them is the one that no one else can ever know."

"That you killed Waylin."

"Aye, my child that is the bit no one must ever know, except you."

"I shall take that secret to the grave."

She turned him and looked him square in the eyes and said, "take this to the grave as well. I did not kill Waylin; I merely hastened him to the grave. Had the events transpired only one day earlier though, it would have been murder. By the time I tended to those wounds, not even a full mage of any element or an Elementalist would have been able to heal them. I am only a storyteller after all with limited knowledge of the healing arts."

"You are more than that and you know it."

"Time will tell."

"What is the next step?"

"Cara and Cedric will help us. I am hoping she will listen to them because they have never lied to her. Cara is walking back the horses you two left at my house this morning and hoping that she will be able to mend some bridges. For now, though you need sleep. I'll keep watch from here."

Aiden nodded and went off to Kiana's house for some much-needed shut-eye. From her vantage point, she saw Ailia come out from the house shortly after he left. She went about her chores like any other day and feeding the animals was first. Then she tended to her growing crops. She noticed that her eyes were puffy yet again and that her hair was messy and uncombed.

, she thought as Cara walked up with both horses.

"Ailia," She called out.

"Good morning, how are you?"

"I'm well and so are the horses. After you ran off last night Cedric and I took them to board in our stables for the night. I thought I would bring them back to you this morning."

Ailia went up to Solas and nuzzled the mare's face before turning to her friend and saying, "Thank you but you really shouldn't have walked all the way here in your condition. I greatly appreciate it and now that you're here, can I offer you a cup of tea?"

"I would love that."

"Let me put these guys in the pasture and then we can go inside."

Cara walked with Ailia to the pasture and helped her lead the horses inside before they headed to the house. Once in the kitchen, Ailia put on a kettle to boil and the pair sat at the table.

"How are you doing with everything," Cara asked.

"To be honest, I am not really sure. Last night had you asked that I would have said I was angry, but now in the light of a new day. Confused, hurt, joyful are all words that come to mind as well."

"So you believe Kiana then?"

"To be honest, I am not sure what to believe. I want to still trust her not to lie to me. I mean, I don't really remember a time when I didn't trust Kiana or think of her as a grandmother. A part of me believes that she would omit things for her own reasons. I guess there are still many things that I need to learn about this world and myself."

"Well take it from someone who was raised by her, You can trust her. I could see the truth in her words yesterday."

"I get that but it's still a lot to work through." Ailia sighed.

"What about Aiden? Can you trust the cute one?" Cara asked as the kettle whistled.

"Him, I'm even less sure about," Ailia said, rolling her eyes at the cute remark. She stood and walked over to grab the kettle from the fire. She set the hot kettle on a pad on the table and then grabbed two cups from the cupboard.

"So what's your next move?"

"I don't have one. I don't need one. I am a simple farm girl and who my parents are or aren't doesn't change that," she said pouring the hot water into the cups before grabbing a handful of tea leaves for the both of them.

"They both had more to say you know."

"Regardless of anything they had to say my choice is the same. I want to take care of my animals and tend to the farm. Survive off the land as long as I am able. I'm sure by now the whole village knows that I am alone in our endeavors. I am sure that will change what they buy from this land. I will do what I have to stay here and run things my way. That's all I have ever wanted and now I can do that free from anyone's influences."

"The village doesn't care that you do all the work that has never mattered to anyone but you. I can understand that you are finally free and want your chance to do it all yourself and I don't want to stop you but I think you should at least finish hearing them out."

"Let me guess you know everything now?"

"Well I don't think one can ever know anything when Kiana is speaking but I do know more than I did when you walked out of the house yesterday."

"I'll have to think about it. I don't know if I want to know anymore."

"What if it could change your life? What if it could change it in the best way possible?"

"That is exactly why I don't want to know anymore. I am happy where I am at," Ailia sighed, stood, and shook her head before saying, "I guess I can consider hearing them out, but only because you asked me too.

"I can appreciate that and also know that no matter what I am always here for you Ailia," Cara said as she finished up her tea and said, "You are family. I hope you know that."

"I know and I consider you and Cedric family as well. You have always been there for me and I am not angry at you or Cedric."

"Now that I do know, I can see how it makes sense though."

"Yeah, it would explain why I never got any love from him and why she always drank," Ailia said and nodded.

The pair sat and talked about the changes Ailia wanted to make to the farm and how the crops were doing and the animals. The sun was high in the sky when Cara finally excused herself and took the long walk back to her home. Ailia checked on the animals and brushed each of the horses down as the sun slowly started to sink into the horizon. Ailia retired early as far as Kiana could see from her vantage point.

As dusk settled Aiden appeared next to Kiana looking refreshed.

"How was today?" He asked.

"Quiet, Cara returned the horses and they talked for a while but no other visitors. Certainly not the ones we fear are coming."

"That is good news, but you should rest Kiana. Cedric said he would take over at dawn."

Kiana nodded and without another word slipped deeper into the woods and took her leave. For the next week, they gave Ailia all the space she wanted but kept a close watch on her. When they thought they had given her enough space Kiana came around midday and approached Ailia as she led one of the horses out of the barn.

"I don't want to talk, Kiana," Ailia said before Kiana could say a single word.

"I know you don't want to and you don't have to talk but you need to listen to the rest of what I have to say."

"Why should I even trust you?"

"I have never lied to you. Yes, there have been things that I have kept from you. I kept them from you for what I believe is a good reason but I have never outright lied to you."

Ailia thought for a second as she led the horse the rest of the way to the pasture, "fine, I will listen," She relented.

"Thank you, Ailia, I told you that you were kidnapped as a baby. That alone would be enough to shock anyone. I know I also mentioned that you still have a family out there. Your parents are still looking for you to this day. They never stopped looking. No one in the Consentori has ever stopped looking for you"

"You said all of that the other day. They did a pretty damn poor job of looking for me. It's not like I was moved every year. I have been here the whole time."

"Oh Ailia, Mynor is a big country. We live in a small part of it."

"Well that I suppose could be a reason," Ailia paused and looked down at the dirt for a few minutes before looking back up at Kiana, "I have been so angry since you told me that I never thought about the possibility of them still being out there. I was too wrapped up losing the only family I thought I had. I didn't want to listen when you told me my parents were still looking for me. I didn't want to think that there might be one waiting for me."

"I know your parents, quite well and your Uncle. Ailia and I know how much hope they placed in Aiden when they sent him to look for you. I also know how much danger you are now in, which is why I held off on telling you."

"Why would I be in danger?"

"Well, there was a reason that you were kidnapped. From everything we have learned you were supposed to be murdered. Forces in Mynor do not want you to know your full potential. They were allowed to keep you alive because you didn't know the truth. Waylin's death and Rhona's attacks have set things in motion and will serve as a signal to the Threnians that you have been made aware of the truth. They will assume that you have chosen the Consentori's side."

Kiana took a breath and in that instant, a loud cracking noise sounded. Ailia looked around and tried to figure out where it had come from. It didn't take long before a masked figure appeared from behind the house yelling. Aiden rushed out to intercept him from the tree line where he had been hiding. The figure was distracted from the women and turned towards Aiden. He threw a punch at him and Aiden evaded the first punch thrown by leaning to the right as he threw a matching blow which landed square on the figures' jaw. This knocked him back and Aiden didn't let up throwing blow after blow.

He struck the figure in the jaw and stomach until he could no longer stand and fell to one knee. Aiden then delivered a powerful roundhouse kick to the side of the head and the figure collapsed into a heap. Kiana and Ailia approached. As they did Aiden bent down and took off the figures mask. It was a young man no more than twenty and his face was covered with weird marks.

"What do those markings mean?" Ailia asked as they got closer.

"The emblem for the Thren is a four-pointed star covered in thorny vines. They call it the 'Constraint of life'. From what the Consentori understand the personal assassins of Drecan Undergallows have the vines marked into their skin and thorns are added with each confirmed kill of a mage."

"It looks like this guy has at least twenty confirmed kills," Aiden said after a quick look at the man's face.

"Why would he be here now?" Ailia asked.

"He is a mage hunter and I am sure that by now the news of Waylin's death has reached the Thren," said Kiana.

"So he was here for Aiden?"

"No child, he was here for you. The Thren would have assumed that you had found out about your origins. I was hoping we would have sometime before the assassins started to show. I was wrong it seems. Looks like Drecan Undergallows is not going to take any chances. He has assumed you have chosen our side. The assassins will not stop until we liberate all of Mynor."

"But I have no magical abilities. Why would he be here for me? Why would my choice make any difference?"

"There is a prophecy that you are a powerful unique type of mage."

Before Kiana could say any more the assassin stirred and Aiden dealt him another punch to the nose and went to find some rope to tie him up. Once that was done Aiden with Ailia's help hoisted him into the wagon and then drove him to the jail. The sheriff jailed him next to Rhona quietly to avoid any commotion. The three continued on to Kiana's house and Aiden fetched Cara and Cedric so the five of them could discuss this most recent attack and what the next steps they needed to take.

Chapter Twelve

"We have been attacked again at the farm. This is only going to keep happening. So we need to come up with a plan of action."

"First off why does this keep happening?"

Kiana stood and walked to her bookcase. She thumbed through a few volumes before turning to the group.

"Found it!" she exclaimed and then read, "When the forest finds its light once more in the eye of a storm, there shall be a single babe born. Within that babe the fate of humanity lies. For if the forest can wield it's full might the world may weather any future storm."

"It is the belief of many within the Thren and within the Cosantóirí that you are this child, Ailia."

"That is why they want me dead because they think I'm a tree?"

"It is more complicated than that. The forest refers to a special type of mage. You are a powerful mage, the most powerful kind. You are an Elementalist."

"I have never been able to use Magick. How can you be so sure that I am this child?"

"One simple thing tells me that you are what the prophecy says you are. It's your eyes, my child."

"My eyes?" Ailia asked, looking doubtful.

"What about her eyes?" Cedric asked looking at Ailia.

"Let me ask you this. Have you ever seen anyone else have green eyes?

"Now that I think about it, no, I haven't" Cara said.

"You know why that is, don't you?"

"No, I don't.

"Elementalists are not like any other mage. Most mages have no outward mark of Magick but Elementalist's eyes change at birth to a bright emerald green."

"So that's the only proof you have?"

"That's all I need. I was there when you were born. It was in the middle of one of the worst storms that has ever hit Mynor in written history. Just as you were born the thunder and lightning stopped. The rain tapered off, all was calm, and you were born. Your eyes were a deep sky blue and then the storm was back worse than before and you cried and your eyes glowed green for an instant as they changed.

"No one realized just how important you would be until the first attempted kidnapping three days after you were born. Your parents took you and went on the run at that point surviving only in the forest. They spent weeks in the woods moving each night to a new place. They occasionally heard whispers in the towns about a baby Elementalist and they worried. It was slow moving through the woods with a newborn but they continued on. It was two days before the end of the rainy season when they decided to take a day's rest and let you get some well needed sleep. Your father had taken the first watch but he was tired after months on the road and dozed off. He awoke as Waylin and Rhona attacked the camp."

"What happened?" Ailia asked.

"That is a story for your parents to tell you for they are the ones that know it the best."

"So if I am this really powerful Elementalist why have my powers never manifested?"

"Waylin and Rhona saw fit to that. Aye, they kept you alive when you were marked but they tried with all their might to hate the love right out of you. You grew up so fast because you had to and there was so little that I could do to protect you. I did what I could to give you the love that you needed."

"So does that mean that love is the answer to being a Mage?"

"No love is only an ingredient and each person's recipe is different. Your powers will come in time as will all things."

A silence crept over the group each one trying to soak in the events of the last two weeks. Ailia tried hard to wrap her mind around that everything was a lie.

She thought and took a deep breath to settle the fluttering of her heart. Aiden watched her through the silence and pondered a great many things as well.

After some time Cedric finally spoke again, "So what is our plan then?"

"There is only one thing that can be done. This town is no longer safe with us in it. We are vulnerable and we put the other villagers who have no conflict with the Thren at risk." Kiana said standing to look outside in the direction of Latzu.

"We must leave," Ailia said.

"Aye, we must but not as one group. Ailia you must go with Aiden as your path is much longer than ours. I will take Cara and

Cedric to the compound. It is there that we shall meet again. There are just a few things we must do first before we leave," Kiana explained

"What things need to be done?" Ailia asked.

"Cara, Cedric," Kiana said looking at them, before continuing, "you must gather only your precious belongings. We meet back here at sundown tonight."

Cara and Cedric both nodded and then took their leave. After they had gone Kiana turned to Aiden. She looked at him and then at Ailia before standing and walking to her mantle.

"You two will have to go at it alone. Your path will be long and rarely easy. It will take you through many heavily occupied areas of Mynor," She said as she rifled through a box on the shelf, "Ailia you must trust Aiden to protect you and Aiden you must remember all of your training and your orders."

They both nodded as Kiana turned around and faced them. She had a scroll in one hand and a satchel in the other. She handed the scroll to Aiden and the pouch to Ailia.

"These will guide you on your travels and keep them close. The map has marked the locations of two of the mages that will need to train you Ailia. They will guide you on your path to realizing your true powers," She turned to Aiden, "The earth mage should be first. It is closest and you shouldn't run into any troops or heavily guarded areas. Her name is Taryn and she will not take kindly to strangers."

Both Aiden and Ailia nodded at her instructions and Kiana continued on, "Now before you leave you must return to the homestead and pack what you want to keep, Ailia, as well as whatever other supplies you can muster. I know you have three horses. It would be wise to use all three. Aiden while she packs you must find whatever communications you can. Any information will be helpful."

"Understood," Aiden said and the pair also took their leave. Kiana sighed as they closed the door behind them. Once alone, she also took stock of her possessions and worked to make ready for the journey.

Chapter Thirteen

Ailia was quite as they made their way back to the homestead. when they got there she went to her room without a word. Aiden frowned and opened the other door and went in not waiting for her to finish packing. He looked around for a few seconds before spotting the desk on the wall next to the door and began to rifle through the drawers and the papers he found. They all looked like land deeds, store receipts; basic records of life.

He sighed and shook his head and then the thought dawned on him,

He paused and looked around again. He opened the closet doors and spotted a box in the bottom corner and picked it up. He placed it on the bed and flicked off the cover. His eyes grew wide at the box's contents. It was full of daggers and other sacrificial items. Aiden recognized one of the small blades and held it up to the light. The embedded red crystals glinted in the sun and his mouth opened slightly as he ran his fingers gently over the handle. He jumped slightly as Ailia cleared her throat from the doorway.

"What are you doing to that knife," Ailia asked her eyebrow raised slightly as his hands traced over the etching in the hilt.

"Look," he pulled his knife from its sheath and handed both to Ailia, "do you see the same rubies and markings?" she nodded and he sighed, "these are Cosantóirí blades. We are awarded them by our leader at the commencement of our training."

"Do you think they took it from my father," she asked quietly.

Aiden simply nodded. Ailia went back to her room not sure what to say. For a third time, he looked at the room over and finally noticed the old worn and well-traveled trunk at the foot of the bed.

Aiden went to it, knelt down, and pushed the top gently open. He riffled through it and then grinned.

thought as he lifted out a smaller box. He dusted off the cover with his sleeve to reveal a strange symbol on the cover. The symbol had 4 points, but it wasn't a cross, it was more like a star. A star covered in thorns.

"This is the box that will have all the answers in it," Aiden relaxed letting a soft glow spread across his face. Ailia heard him and walked back into the room.

"What is that thing?"Ailia pointed to the symbol, "It is like a weird star."

"That's the 'Constraint of Life'. This is where those weird marks come from. The one from the assassins face."

Ailia's eyes softened and he started to read the letters and notes written on scraps of folded paper. Within the box, there were countless orders for different jobs, hits, and other petty things but none of these would mean much to Ailia. They didn't pertain to her or anyone she knew. Then he spotted it lying on the bottom of the box. He pulled out the paper and looked it over. The note was creased like it had been folded and unfolded several thousand times. Over time the parchment had yellowed and became slightly brittle. It also looked as if it had spent some time under a cup of tea, but the writing was a dark thick black ink and thankfully still readable.

He handed the paper over to Ailia. She read it softly, "She will be the only babe with green eyes, for miles. Her parents have been reported to be traveling in the woods by night, trying to make their way to an outpost no doubt," Ailia closed her eyes for a moment to take a deep breath before reading on, "The babe has a small heart shaped birthmark on her right shoulder" Ailia gasped as tears formed in her eyes her hand grabbed her shoulder and rubbed it gently, her voice caught as she read on, "when you find her

her," she looked up at Aiden and tried to speak but nothing came out. Her eyes darted back to the letter and she read it several times until she looked at him again and mouthed 'me'.

Aiden nodded shuffling through the box until he found a second letter and sighed, "This explains why you're still alive," he looked up from the paper and noticed her still crying so he asked, "Shall I read it?" Ailia nodded as the tears ran from her eyes like waterfalls and Aiden started softly, "Waylin – it is regrettable that your wife has taken to the babe and so have you I am told. I understand that she has even named it Ailia Rain. That wasn't the plan. I should have your head for this; however, you have proved useful in the past so I am willing to be generous. Raise her as your own for now and ensure her sympathies lie with me. I don't want her knowing the truth. If we can I shall use her as a weapon and kill her when the war is won. If not I shall kill her before she has the chance to do any harm. ~Drecan,"

Ailia stood there for a moment before saying, "I believed you and Kiana when you told me, but I guess there was still a part of me that didn't want to believe it all. At least not until you read that."

"I know it's hard, Ailia. I can't begin to imagine how startling all of this is for you."

Ailia ignored his comment and said, "We have to keep moving. You should go out to the workshop who knows what is hidden out there. I have to finish packing."

Aiden nodded and went out to the barn and Ailia headed into her room. She grabbed her old rusty colored knapsack with a few sets of traveling clothes, her leather hunting pants, a heavy jacket, and an old blanket that she used when hunting. She paused and thought for a second before dumping her pack out. She repacked the clothes on the bottom but left the blanket out.

. She put the old one back in her trunk. Sighing she grabbed a small box from under her bed and flicked it open. Inside she could see her knife and her flint and steel. She packed those and then cataloged in her head what she still needed to grab. From under her bed, she grabbed her water skin and from behind the door, she grabbed her quiver full of arrows and her bow.

She stood with the soft leather water skin hanging limply from her hand and looked around. She dropped the water skin; it thumped softly as it hit the bed landing near the small empty box that had held her knife. She set the bow and quiver down next to it. Next, Ailia turned and walked the few steps to her trunk and knelt down to open it again. She pushed her old blanket aside and frowned, finding her bundle of rope.

she wondered as she grabbed it. She stood just as a gust of air wiped though her room, making her hair fly. She turned, slightly on edge, expecting Aiden to pop his head in. She dropped the rope on her way to look out both of her windows. She sighed when she found nothing strange outside.

Shaking it off, She pulled her head back inside, her eyes fell on her half-full pack and the reality of what she was doing hit her. Tears welled up in her eyes and broke free racing down her cheeks as she sank down onto the floor drawing her knees to her chest.

Ailia's mind wailed as she rubbed her temples, tears still flowing freely from her eyes. She sat like that as the wind whipped outside.

She thought as she sniffled and wiped her eyes a few times. The cold breeze blew through again and a shiver ran down her spine. 'You work through the pain' she could remember Kiana telling her one day after a particularly bad fight with Waylin. Ailia weakly smiled at the thought of Kiana and slowly pushed herself up off the floor.

Ailia went back to her pack and sighed. She put all the items she had collected into her knapsack and then changed into a pair of pants and a long sleeve undershirt with a sleeveless top over it. She sat at her desk and tied bracers onto her forearms. She sighed again and pulled her boots on before strapping her knife to her ankle. Around her neck, she hung a small blue pouch with delicate beadwork. Kiana gave her in her fifteenth year. Ailia sighed and double checked the knots on her bracers before slipping on her jacket. She grabbed her gem pouch and fastened it to her belt before shoving it into the pocket of her pants.

she kept telling herself. With this mindset, she finished packing and braiding her hair. She tied her hair off as a ray of dusky sunshine poked through the grey and angry clouds and painted her room in a reddish-golden glow. The sun made her smile softly as she relaxed and walked to the window. When she rested her hands on the sill she cried a single tear at the glint that shone from her ring finger. She sighed and looked at the silver filigree that surrounded the burgundy stone of someone she never knew.

Ailia slid the ring off her finger and set it on the desk and shed a few tears.

Instead of letting the tears consume her she continued to work willing them to stay at bay. She rolled up her blanket and strapped to her pack. She looked at her bed and saw the empty box and picked it up as she sat on the bed. She grabbed her knife from its home on her ankle and used it to slice the lining of the box. She put her knife back and fished on the inside of the box for a few seconds before pulling out a green pendant. She dangled it from her hand as she thought

She slipped the pendant into her pocket and turned back to her desk

She saw the silver ring now dull as the clouds swallowed the sun up and grabbed it.

She braided it into her hair. Ailia took a look at the four walls and the windows that were her life and sighed. She walked to the window by her bed and looked out with one deep breath she had made up her mind.

Chapter Fourteen

Aiden dug through the workshop and found a few more boxes of intelligence. He stacked these up and was finishing up his search as Ailia walked out of the house with her pack. She didn't say much but went to the supply room and started to saddle up the horses. She saddled Solas first with an extra set of saddlebags, then Iasair, also with extra bags, and lastly she saddled up the other stallion Talam. Ailia also added several pack bags to the Talam. In one of those bags, she packed the grooming necessities for the horses. She also packed a few other extras including a few more lengths of rope and some of her favorite tools like her shears. She then went back inside and pulled out all of the dried and cured meat from the cellar. Aiden helped her load the meat into the saddlebags and then helped her carry up some of the other preserved food like vegetables they had canned last season.

Ailia took one last look around and grabbed a few more items she thought might be helpful on the journey. She then tethered Talam to Solas with a sturdy rope and mounted her horse. Aiden mounted Iasair and they left. As they started on the path towards town Ailia looked back and thought,

As the farm disappeared from view and the closer they got to town Ailia shed a few tears. They went through town and Ailia stopped off at the market to settle her account and arrange for the animals to be sold and taken care of. They hoped by making it clear that Ailia was leaving the Thren wouldn't send any further troops or assassins looking for her. Ailia didn't want to endanger anyone else's left because of her choices.

While she took care of things at the market Aiden continued on to Kiana's house with Iasair. He dismounted the horse and tied him up walking inside. There he found Kiana packing. She looked up from her bag as he entered.

"Are you ready," Aiden asked.

She walked over to the window and looked out at the brilliant reddish glow coming from the west, "The sun is setting. Where is Ailia? I thought she would be with you." Kiana asked Aiden as the rays of sunset warmed her body and brought peace and understanding to her heart.

"She is at the market, selling off what we aren't taking with us. Mainly the animals. I don't think she could ever just leave them. It's not in her nature to let them go untaken care of. We both hope it will also deter the Thren from looking here. Neither of us wants anyone else getting hurt."

"This journey will not be an easy one for either of you. There are some things that I think you should have to help you," Kiana said as she turned from the sunset glow and walked back towards Aiden. She walked over to one of her shelves and from a decorative box she pulled out a roll of fabric tied with a thick leather strip. She also grabbed a talisman from the shelf as well. Turning back to Aiden, Kiana handed them both to him.

"You'll need the talisman when speaking with the mages it will prove the mission you are on. Without it, I fear she will never have the training she needs. As for the other thing, these are my throwing knives. You will probably have more luck with them, though I hope you never need to use them."

Aiden thanked her and went outside to place the new items into his pack. When he returned Kiana was gazing at the dancing fire.

"Now we are just waiting for the sun to sink and for Ailia to finish up in town. I know Cara and Cedric are going with you but after we leave can you round up the other members, especially any mages who may be hiding here. Even with Ailia cutting ties, they are still at risk from the Thren."

"I will," Kiana said and went back to packing.

"They might want to head there as well. It won't be safe here anymore, not with the trouble her leaving will stir up," he paused and looked at her and she nodded softly.

"What kind of intelligence did you find at the farm? Anything useful?"

"Most of this is about old missions but there is a lot of it. I'm hoping command can make more sense of it. I did find the missives explaining why she wasn't killed and the initial order to kidnap her. I let her read one and I think that took care of that last bit of doubt I felt she still had."

"Aye, I can see why that would. Did you find anything else of value when searching?"

"I did find one of our blades. I'm thinking it's her fathers. I took that.

"Did you find anything else? A necklace by chance, I am hoping?"

"No, there wasn't any necklace. Were you hoping there would be?"

"Yes, I was hoping you would find one. When she was taken there was a green pendant around her little neck that her father had given her at birth. He told me one time it was a family thing something passed down from his mother. I was hoping that it would be recovered but I guess not."

"I am sorry but there was nothing like that, and I searched everywhere I could at the farm. Maybe we should ask Ailia if she ever saw anything like that." Aiden said with a sigh.

"Maybe but I'm not sure what if it hurts her worse to lose something else that was hers," Kiana sighed looking troubled.

"Damned if we do and damned if we don't I guess," he said and walked over to stir the fire causing it to dance and the smoke to form a likeness of Ailia.

"You're falling for her and I don't blame you, she is a wonderful girl."

"No Kiana I'm not. It's just a mission. I'm more professional than that," Aiden swiped away the image of Ailia and turned to face Kiana his face set with a slight grimace, "get the members out."

Kiana chucked softly giving him a knowing look before replying, "I'll get them out, I promise."

"That includes you and don't give me any excuses."

"And why do you think I should go there?" she asked, picking up her knitting to pack.

"You're too old to take chances and besides you know upper management always needs your help I'm surprised the base runs without you. In fact, it might run without you but we are so much more efficient with your keen eyes there to guide us through our blunders," Aiden whispered softly.

"You are too kind though my age shouldn't worry you. I am not nearly as old as I look, young one. Besides one is only old if they let themselves be. I wonder where you get your sense of kindness and duty from. It's certainly not your mother."

Aiden laughed, "I forget you barely got to know my father, but if you had I'm sure you'd see I am most definitely more like him then I am my mother. You're just lucky you never met my brother. He is a handful."

"Well maybe next time history repeats itself I shall have that chance," Kiana sighed and looked out the window, "Here comes Ailia now. Just in time, the sun is getting rather low."

Ailia walked in looking exhausted and went straight towards Kiana. The two hugged trying to forget the pain of the last few days.

"Ailia, my child, I know that you are hurting now. I can tell you are anxious to get on the road. The sun has set on one chapter of your life but it has not completely faded from your life. It will rise again and happiness will find you again but only when you let your heart open to it," she spoke in a whisper so just Ailia could hear her as Aiden paced on the other side of the room.

"Ah, Aiden, I know you are uneasy with the tasks set upon you now," Kiana spoke louder and he turned his head towards the women listening intently, "but you cannot afford to waver now. Every aspect of your journey must go according to plan and you must get her there safely. That is your only concern. Go and ready the horses now you should leave soon before the sun comes again. I will send Ailia out shortly."

"Of course, Kiana," Aiden responded as he bowed, and backed out of the room. A few seconds later there was a light bang as the old wooden door hit its frame as he left the women in silence to speak.

"Ailia," Kiana said as the door banged shut, "I know you hate us for what we did but it was needed with the proof Aiden found there really was no other choice."

"I know, Kiana and I don't hate you. I never could. I was just upset. I am sorry for how I acted. Did you know Aiden would come eventually?" Ailia asked.

"There are many things I know and many I have yet to learn."

"That isn't an answer Kiana," Ailia protested.

"Everything will answer itself in time, my child but for now let us not be concerned with the past but look only to what lies ahead on your journey."

"Do you think he regrets it?" Ailia asked knowing Kiana wouldn't give her any more information about her past.

"Child, I know he does, as do I. This task wasn't an easy one. He didn't want to hurt you and nor do I but we all have a job to do. Promise me you won't make it any more difficult than it already is for him."

"I promise I will try...," Ailia whispered as tears started to spill from her eyes, "Can I trust him, Kiana?"

"You must, with all of your life, child," Kiana answered as she wiped Ailia's tears away.

"I don't want to leave you," Ailia hugged her tightly.

"You must my child," Kiana smiled at her and held her face in a wrinkled hand, "do not fret about me. I am wise beyond my years with a few tricks up my sleeves yet. I promise you will see me again."

"Alright then, I guess this is goodbye for now," Ailia whispered and started to walk out the door, she turned and said, "Make sure Cara, the baby, and Cedric are safe."

"I will make sure they are," Kiana said and paused for a moment, "Wait, my child, I have something for you before you go."

Kiana rose and walked over to the mantle where a small ashen chest rested. She took a small brass key from a chain around her neck and opened the chest. Inside was another smaller box. Kiana took it out and handed it to Ailia.

"Take this, my child; it will be well needed in your travels."

"What is it?"

"You will see when the time comes the box will open itself for you. Its contents will be of great assistance to you."

"What about you? Will you make sure that Cara and Cedric are safe? I still worry about them, the whole town, everything."

"Of course I will do what I can to make everyone safe, Ailia, but you must not linger anymore."

Ailia nodded and the two walked out the door together. Outside Aiden was talking with Cedric and Cara. Ailia made her goodbyes short so she wouldn't start crying and decide to stay. She knew that she must trust that she would see them again. Aiden mounted first and then Ailia and they disappeared into the woods with the three horses in tow.

They rode north for hours traveling deep into the forest towards their first destination. Solas, Iasair, and Talam trotted through the forest with grace as they jumped over fallen branches and narrow streams. Occasionally they would stop so the horses could drink but mainly they just rode. They rode first towards an unknown for both of them and then eventually to a place Aiden called home. A place Ailia had never known.

Chapter Fifteen

At first, the tears came quietly as they rode through the familiar forest but as the trees flew past and the forest became unknown to her, she slowly felt her tears dry up as if a new reality was slowly replacing the one torn from her. They rode on through the bright moonlight for hours until dawn approached bringing with it the first gleams of light that pierced the loose canopy above. When the sun had been out for a couple hours Aiden slowed their pace slightly.

He spoke the first words since Kiana's house, "let's find a clearing and rest awhile."

Ailia ignored him as they rode on in silence. As they carried on Ailia began to think about all that had happened.
She asked herself. When she began to get tired sometime later she pulled Solas's reins and the horse stood stalled a few paces from Aiden. It didn't take him long to look back at her and frown. He stopped Iasair and turned in the saddle towards her staring at her.

They stared each other down as he thought
he surmised,

"We need either to rest or to keep moving," he said as he spurred Iasair gently and continued on. After a few seconds, she spurred on Solas and followed him. She let a heavy veil of quiet surround them and refused to acknowledge any of his attempts to start a conversation.

she argued with herself but she knew it was more than that. She knew in her heart that she didn't know what to say or where they would go from here.

, She thought,

Soon they came upon a small clearing no more than ten yards wide and almost twice that in length. The clearing was scattered with leaves, twigs and a few young saplings and seemed to be forgotten by everything.

Aiden dismounted and looked around at the old dense trees around the edge of the clearing. He couldn't make out anything past two trees deep into the forest, so he cleared his throat and announced, "This should work just fine if you agree."

Instead of giving him an answer, Ailia jumped down from Solas and landed in a crouch before straightening out and grabbing a slender metal t-post from Talam's larger saddle bag. Aiden looked at her quizzically until she pushed it into the ground. When it was sturdy she led Solas to the post and tied the horse there. She then grabbed Iasair from Aiden and did the same; she also detached the tether from Solas and anchored Talam to the rod as well. Refusing to look or talk to Aiden she went about making camp as he stood there dumbfounded at her.

She stared past him as angry words filled her head. Ailia fumed silently as she cleared a fair size hole in the middle of the small meadow.

Aiden wasn't sure how to help and she was ignoring him so he trudged off into the woods. Ailia let out a sigh.

, she thought as she went around the clearing collecting the random dry leaves strewn about the ground. She piled them in the middle of her makeshift camp before walking around to grab a dozen or so twigs to start a fire.

As she was walking through the clearing she spotted some flat stones and picked them up as well thinking that they would make decent plates while on the road. She set them next to the pile of dead leaves, before heading back around still looking for twigs. Finally the pile of sparse leaves and thin twigs was enough kindling to start a fire all she needed was a few larger twigs that would burn longer.

She went up to a large ash tree and picked off some of the smaller branches and brought them back. Laying them in a loose teepee around the pile of leaves she squatted down and pulled her pack close. She pulled out her flint and steel and struck them together in a shower of radiant sparks that caught the dry leaves ablaze.

She frowned and backed away as the fire lapped at the kindling devouring it like a hungry animal. As the flames danced around the wood Ailia slowly backed away until she could no longer feel the heat. She stood and saw Aiden standing on the edge of the clearing with a half dozen or so logs in his arm and walked back to the horses ignoring him. He sighed and put some of the logs on the fire. He looked up at Ailia and noticed that she was unsaddling the horses.

"What are you doing to them?"

"Did the six months on the farm teach you nothing?" She asked and then not waiting for his response told him, "They need to be brushed and watered especially if they are being ridden like we did today and I expect we intend to for quite some time," she responded curtly as she heaved Solas' saddle off. She carried it back towards Aiden and set it down a yard or so away from the fire. She did the same with the other two saddles.

She put those Saddles on the opposite side of hers. She grabbed a brush from one of the saddlebags and walked back to the horses. She started to brush Solas as she let the silent veil from before creep over the clearing. She focused only on the way the brush felt in her hand and rhythm of the Solas' breathing. The constant motion let her relax and the worries she was feeling floated away for a moment.

"We will only stay here only long enough to rest," Aiden said to her as he sat on Iasair's saddle.

"Fine," Ailia spoke shortly.

"Are you always going to be this sullen?" he asked.

Ailia looked at him and rolled her eyes before going back to brushing Solas.

"Well, are you?" He asked as he pushed off against the saddle and walked towards her.

"Why don't you take a guess?" she replied as he rested his hand on Iasair's flank.

"Gotcha," he sighed and stared at the ground muttering something before he looked back at her, "did you pack any food?"

"Yeah I grabbed some stuff from the homestead but tonight I'll hunt. I only want to use that when we can't find other food."

"Oh… that makes sense"

"Here you finish brushing the horses," she quipped as she pushed the brush into his hand and she strode past him to grab her bow, "I'll go hunt."

Ailia quickly slung her quiver across her back and with her bow in hand darted into the forest and left Aiden with the horses. Iasair looked at him and neighed softly.

Laughing Aiden responded, "Yeah I know," he brushed the horse's neck, "I've made a real mess of it, haven't I? All that time I took getting to know her. Getting her to trust me seems to all be for not."

Solas joined the conversation with a loud snicker.

"How would you have done it?"

Both Solas and Iasair turned and looked away from Aiden

Talam, however, nudged his hand looking for something to snack

on.

"Yeah, that's what I thought," Aiden muttered to himself as

he went back to brushing the horses. The soft strokes against the

horse's neck calmed him down and let him think.

He finished brushing all of the horses and put the brush back

in one of the saddlebags. Not sure what else to do Aiden sat down by

Iasair's saddle and waited for her return. He watched the fire and

smoke dance up towards the sky. A while later Ailia returned with

two limp rabbits and a squirrel on her shoulder.

"What's up with the squirrel?" Aiden asked as she sat down

on her side of the fire.

"He's a friend."

"A friend? But it's a squirrel" Aiden asked, raising an

eyebrow as he picked a blade of grass twirling it in his fingers.

"If you can talk to my horses; I can have a squirrel for a

friend. Oh and just so you know he prefers McLeod, not squirrel."

Ailia smiled smugly at the dumbfounded look on Aiden's face as

McLeod jumped from her shoulder and watched Ailia skinned and cleaned the rabbits.

Aiden joined McLeod in watching Ailia work carefully with her hunting knife as she made quick work of the rabbits and in no time the meat was deboned and lying in a pile on one of the skins.

Ailia looked up at him when she was done and pointed to the flat rocks she found earlier. She commanded, "Grab those and come with me."

She stood and then walked towards the horses untying them with McLeod following and scampering up Solas's braided tail. The horse tried to swat the squirrel off until the Ailia steadied the horse with her hand.

She led them to the right disappearing into the woods. Aiden grabbed the stones and followed. She led him to a stream not more than five minutes from camp. Ailia let the horses drink. Aiden stared at her.

"Well, aren't you going to wash the stones? Or were you raised by a pack of wolves?" Ailia snipped at him as she bent over and filled her water skin. She stood and took a few drinks before replacing them again and screwing on the cap. She then reattached her skin to her belt and retook the horses' reins.

Aiden blushed but walked to the stream and knelt down scrubbing the dirt off of the stones. It took him a while but soon the stones were dirt free. He showed them to Ailia and she gave him a small nod before pulling on all of the horses' reins and walking away leaving him there in silence.

he thought to himself as he walked back to the small clearing;

When Aiden got back to the clearing Ailia had moved her saddle farther from the fire and was cleaning her knife with an old cloth. He walked up to her and offered her the stones.

Looking up at him, she remarked, "So I have to do all the work I see."

She grabbed the stones from him and went to the fire. With a long stick, she made indents in the ashes and laid them down.

"Wait," Aiden whispered as he put his hand on her arm as she walked towards the rabbit meat, "I can cook the meat."

"Fine…," Ailia responded and took off the pouch around her neck, "here use this. There are some good spices inside." Aiden grabbed the pouch as she moved out of his way.

"You know, I am sorry," Aiden said as he divided the meat out on the stones.

"For what?" Ailia asked.

"Ya know, sort of ruining your life back there, If I hadn't shown up you could have lived out the rest of your life a farm girl like you wanted to be. Instead of being stuck here with me…" Aiden trailed off as he sprinkled some salt and other spices over the meat.

"Whatever it's too late for sorry. Just tell me how long until I can be free of you?"

"Well if you want the truth," Aiden paused and she nodded her head, "You're sort of stuck with me for the rest of your life…"

"What do you mean the rest of my ?" Ailia groaned and stood walking over to the far edge of the clearing. McLeod followed her and scampered up to her shoulder. When Aiden started talking she turned her head towards him slightly to listen.

"My mission isn't just to rescue you, I have also been charged with being your protector. Being a protector is a serious assignment and they don't hand them out easily. You received one because your life determines the outcome of the war. I was chosen as the person best suited to protect our only hope. They also thought it would be less traumatic for you if you had a new constant in your life after everything that was torn away," Aiden quietly responded as he took his knife out. He used the blade to flip the meat over as it seared away on the hot stones.

Ailia let out a puff of air and sighed.

She turned to the forest and sighed as McLeod put a paw on her face. She smiled at him and then faced Aiden. Slowly she walked back to her saddle and sat down in front of it renewing her vow of silence. She watched the meat sizzle as she leaned back against the saddle.

She let herself get lost in the hisses as the juices from the rabbit was super-heated by the flames licking the air around the stones. She caught herself smiling as she watched the flames dance in Aiden's eyes and for a moment she could see that he really was sorry. The wind shifted and smoke drifted towards her. She shielded her eyes and coughed as her sour mood returned. She tilted her head away from the flames and scanned the tree lines watching a pair of birds flit to and fro. She appreciated their beauty and continued to watch them getting lost in their dance.

"The meat is done," Aiden announced, using the stick to carefully push the stones away from the heat.

Ailia turned her head from the birds and returned them to the fire. As she waited for the stones to cool she sighed and looked at the ground.

"Are you ever going to talk?" he asked.

"Not really."

"Your life is going to be awfully quiet then."

Ailia hissed at him as she grabbed a loaf of bread from her pack and sliced him a piece using the knife from her ankle. She threw it at him and luckily for Aiden he caught it. He put some of the cooked meat onto the piece of bread and took a bite. As they ate, clouds rolled in covering the sinking sun with a bleak chilling darkness. Ailia looked up at the sky, the cool air making her skin prickle and then sighed softly.

she thought as she finished the last piece of rabbit.

When she had finished she took her stone to the stream and washed it carefully. Aiden followed shortly after. While he was washing his stone, Ailia made her way back to camp. She took the rabbit pelts and strung them to a tree to dry while they rested. When the pelts were hung she took the rest of the rabbit carcasses deep into the forest so no animals would find their camp.

She made her way back to her saddle and grabbed her blanket cuddling up with it as Aiden came back from the stream. She ignored him and closed her eyes. In minutes she was sleeping, her quiet peaceful breathing filled the air as her body took some much-needed rest. He placed his stone on top of hers and sighed. He sat down near his saddle and watched as the fire licked slowly at the logs. He took a good look at the surroundings of the camp keeping an eye out for movement.

Slowly his eyes turned towards Ailia once more. He could just barely make out her face in the fire glow. She was curled up tightly with McLeod by her side. Aiden smiled as he watched the gentle rise and fall of her chest.

he thought to himself as he grabbed a twig from the edge of the fire and started to whittle it down with his knife.

Chapter Sixteen

At least she is still peaceful, he thought a few hours later as

he watched the dim light from the slowly dying fire dance on her

face. As the fire turned to nothing but embers, he slowly began to

drift off, his eyelids becoming heavy veils over his chestnut brown

eyes. He struggled to keep his eyes open as he tried to scan the forest

again. Seeing nothing out of the ordinary, he let himself drift off as

the last embers of the fire fizzled out and died.

Aiden was asleep for no more than a few minutes when a

large crack echoed in the sky startling him awake. He bolted upright

as the noise became louder. The horses were pawing at the ground as

Aiden got to his feet. The rain had started to fall at a steady rate.

he asked himself,

. He walked over to Ailia and knelt down to wake her so they could

take cover. The thunder rang through the camp again. He looked

down at her and realized the rain was coming from her. That it was a

painful sob being ripped from her chest.

thought and gently took hold of her shoulders to shake her from her

slumber. He wanted to stop her pain so as he shook her he softly cooed, "It's alright I won't let anyone hurt you. You're safe with me."

Slowly her eyes fluttered open still brimming with tears and she looked up at him. She didn't say anything but her eyes bored into him demanding to know why.

"Ailia, you should know," Aiden said as he sat down next to her, "I never meant to hurt you and although I know I did hurt you it wasn't because I wanted you to suffer. I was … I still am trying to stop your pain."

"I'm supposed to trust you," she muttered as she sat up.

Aiden put an arm around her shoulders and gently whispered, "I hope that you will trust me, not because you were told to but because you actually do, and I hope that you trust me with your life, and trust that I'm doing what is really best for you. I know it won't be easy but maybe one day you can trust me like you trusted me before all of this happened."

"So you're really here just to protect me?" she asked tears still streaming down her face as she rested one cheek on Aiden's shoulder.

"Yes Ailia," he whispered softly as he wiped her tears away.

"Okay, then," Ailia responded and looked up at him with a soft smile.

"Are you going to be okay now?"

"I think so," Ailia said nodding as she sat up and looked at him, "how long was I out?"

"A few hours, I think. Are you ready to move out?"

"Did you get any sleep?"

"Nah, I'm good though," Aiden said as he stretched before walking back over by his saddle.

"Okay... I guess," Ailia said with a sigh, "You sure?"

Aiden just nodded as he stood and saddled Iasair. A silence crept over them as they broke down camp, but it wasn't an awkward one like before but rather a silence of comfort. It didn't take them long before they were once again headed north.

"What's the compound like?"

"Home," Aiden answered softly, a wistful gleam touching his eyes as he grabbed a twig from a passing tree and started playing with it as he talked while they rode.

"You miss it don't you?" she observed quietly as she petted McLeod.

"Yeah, believe it or not, this is only like the fourth or fifth time I've ever been away from it for more than a few hours."

"Really, and you're how old?"

"Twenty and Four…"

"Wow… only five times?"

"Yeah, once when I was ten and three I went to a battle… My father died on that trip. Then there is this trip and a couple other shorter training exercises," he told her as they rode.

"You were so young…"

"Would you like to hear the story," he paused and waited for her to nod. It took her a few seconds but she did and he continued on, "my father was a Cosantóirí officer just like I am now. Well back before he died, I didn't want to be an officer. I didn't really want anything to do with the war, to be honest. I guess I just didn't have the killer instinct to be a foot soldier and work my way up."

"I can see that you have very little killer instinct," Ailia interrupted and smiled before motioning him to go on.

"And well my papa knew that so a year prior to his death when we had to choose between me going to the military school or civic works academy. Papa let me go to the civic works.

He still wanted me to have a killer instinct so he would keep trying to convince me to travel with him on missions and to see battles. I guess he wanted me to know what he did and why and understand it all even though I was only eleven at the time. I finally gave in and went to a battle," Aiden paused momentarily and took a deep breath before continuing, "My dad and I were up on a ridge looking down at the battle and he was shouting orders. The Thren ambushed a portion of our troops and we were losing so many men that my father jumped on his horse and sped down to help.

"A Threnian archer hit him in the arm but he kept riding on to help his men. That's the kind of man he was. He never abandoned anyone who needed his help. I guess I turned into that kind of man too now that I think about it. I hope I've made him proud." Aiden trailed off momentarily choked at the thought of his father.

Ailia let the silence hover for a few moments and then cleared her throat, "so what happened after your father was shot in the arm?"

Aiden cleared his throat and went on, "Well, being the general that he was a little arrow could not stop him. He kept on riding into the fight. When he got down there he took out his sword and started to push back the Thren. While fighting he took a few more hits and dealt out many more blows to the enemy. His presence and his will to fight inspired the soldiers and we rallied back against them slowly crushing the ambush we had almost dispatched of all the enemy troops when a group of ten soldiers attacked Papa. While he was dealing with them until a Threnian horseman came up alongside him. I don't think my father even knew there was danger but that horseman lopped off my father's head."

"Did we still defeat the ambush, or did the men just quit without their leader?" Ailia asked as they continued to ride.

"We almost did lose. After papa was gone the soldiers continued to fight but their heart was lost in sorrow. The Threnians saw this and sent back the same horseman that had killed my dad. They sent him back to collect more heads for them. The Threnian put the heads on pikes. The last of the Threnian army took those pikes as war banners and charged at our troops. When our men saw this disgrace, they found their hearts once more and pushed back even harder squashing the ambush completely without another soul lost.

"We took no prisoners and piled their dead and burnt them before we left. You could see the smoke tower for miles away. In my sadness I shaped that smoke tower into a giant version of my father and sent it floating towards the capital for all to see. I didn't get to see Drecan's face when it reached him but I hope he cringed that day when he learned of the defeat," Aiden spat angrily as his hate for the Thren boiled in his body almost overflowing. Ailia could see smoke rising from his body as the anger flowed through him. Aiden broke the twig he had been holding onto and took a deep breath, letting go of the smoke which drifted for a second behind him before disappearing into the air.

Aiden took one more deep breath to settle himself and then continued on, "after the enemy was burned we took our dead and carried them to a field on the edge of the battlefield. That is where we buried them, including Papa, with full military honors and grieved for their sacrifice."

"Why?"

"That is our tradition. I don't know how it started but that's what I have been raised to always do. When I returned my Mammon moved into the widows' corridor with the other ladies who had lost

husbands and told me that I was going to the barracks no matter
what my wishes were. She said that I had to change because I needed
to honor my father just like my brother was already doing."

"That's so sad…"

"Yeah I suppose but life moves on I guess. Everyone handles
grief in their own way and it's easier now looking back then it was
then living through it. So I listened to Mammon, reluctantly and
went to the barracks. My instructors saw the same lacking my father
had. They had two choices. They could have rode me hard and beat a
killer instinct into me or they could give me an opportunity to do
intelligence. In my father's memory, they chose to give me the
opportunity to switch from foot soldier to intelligence or as we call it
Eolas, and I did. I excelled in that program and finished training in
record time. It only took me a little over 5 years compared to the
normal nine and a half."

"Is that why they sent you to rescue me over someone else?"

"Well part of it was because I excelled through training but it
also has to do with me being smart enough to adapt and deal with
people, plus I do have a bit of a killer instinct. It grew some after
Papa died. Mainly it was because I pleaded for the assignment."

"Pleaded?"

"Truth be told, my older brother, who has much more of a killer instinct was sent some five years back while I was still in training and he was obviously unsuccessful. It took him three years to return to base and he brought back an Elementalist for sure but it just wasn't you."

Ailia rode in silence for a bit before asking, "Was Latzu the first place you looked for me?"

"No, I've been out searching for over a year now. My trip took me to a lot of different small towns in the countryside and other remote places. We figured if you were alive that they wouldn't have you in a big city just in case your powers showed. I had almost given up and was in a pub grabbing a bite to eat when I overheard some traveling merchants. They talked about a farm that produced the best vegetables they had tasted in such large amounts they were surprised it was run by a family of only three people. They also mentioned that one of them had eyes like they had never seen. Green as the tree leaves after a heavy rain they said. I looked into it and finally found you."

"Oh…"

As the conversation lulled they continued north through the woods. It was slow going without a marked path to follow. As the forest thickened, Ailia was forced to walk and guide both Solas and Talam over the uneven ground. Ailia didn't mind the extra time it took because it gave her an opportunity to appreciate the new scenery she had never seen before. The trees looked similar but their color was different. Instead of the bright green, she was used to these trees were much darker green. Ailia also noticed that some of the trees were even red and yellow. This went on until they came upon a river in front of a mountain range. Aiden pulled out the map that Kiana had given them. Based on the map, Aiden turned Iasair to the right. He slowed to a stop at the river.

"Any suggestions on how we should cross the river?" Aiden asked.

"Well, we should find a shallow section of the river. As long as it's not too deep and the current is calm we should be able to just walk right across.

Aiden nodded and stripped down to just his pants leaving his shirt and boots by the banks of the river. He walked into the river. He only made it about fifty paces before he hit a sharp drop. He swam back and tried further upstream. He tried again but still hit the same drop off. He tried downstream also with no success so he headed back to shore.

While he had been searching for the shallows Ailia had busied herself making camp and a small fire was burning when he returned. He grabbed a dry pair of pants from his saddlebag. He changed in the woods and laid his wet pants near the fire.

"There aren't any shallows in this part of the river. I'm not sure about our next move. We must cross the river by tomorrow morning. I don't want to stay in one location too long."

"We should head upstream a bit and see if we can find any."

"Well, I don't want to go too far out of our way."

"We may not have a choice. It will take more than a day to make a strong enough of a raft to cross here with horses."

Aiden nodded. Soon his pants were dry and they quickly broke camp and headed further up the rivers' edge. It took them several hours before they happened upon a section of river with a wide shore. Ailia jumped down from her horse and walked out into the river. The water lapped at her feet and up to her mid-calf. She walked back to Aiden and grabbed Solas's reins. Holding them tightly she started to cross the river. Aiden followed her out into the river behind Talam.

Ailia led them slowly across the river. They had made it halfway across when Aiden heard a slight twang of a bow. He turned his head just in time to see an arrow whiz by and land in the water where Ailia had just been.

Chapter Seventeen

"We're under attack," he shouted as he quickly mounted Iasair. Ailia followed his lead and they galloped across the rest of the river. They made their way into the forest as the attackers emerged from the woods behind them.

The group of men wore ragged clothes and Aiden could see that their bow and arrows looked to be cobbled together. He thought to himself.

"They aren't Threnian," Aiden called out to Ailia over the shouts coming from the archers.

"Is that good?" she asked as she tried to coax the horses to go faster through the woods.

Aiden nodded his head just as an arrow clipped Ailia's left thigh. She screamed out in pain as the shallow gash began to trickle blood down her thigh. Ailia's vision shimmered with green and suddenly her skin began to prickle. She could feel the air start to thicken. Then her eyes flashed up to Aiden as more arrows were launched at them. Ailia looked at the archers and then back at Aiden a feverish wish running through her head.

She thought frantically

As her fear grew so did a prickle on her skin. She could feel the air shimmer around her.

They fired another volley but this time instead of flying past them the arrows got stuck in mid-air a few yards behind the horses on the edge of the water. It was like they were suspended in a thick invisible liquid and then one by one their shafts slowly dissolved and the arrowheads dropped into the river and drifted away. The archers looked confused and fired again but it seemed nothing would fly past that point and slowly they disbanded as Aiden and Ailia made it deeper into the woods.

When they had reached a clearing, Ailia looked at Aiden and started to ask what just happened when her eyes rolled back in her head and she slumped against the neck of Solas and started to slide off the horse. Aiden dismounted just in time to catch her as she fainted. He laid her on the ground and began to dig into his pack and took out an old towel. He ripped a strip off from it and tied it tightly above the gash in Ailia's leg. As the bleeding slowed he lit the tip of his finger and used the flame to cauterize the wound. Within a few minutes, her eyes fluttered open and she looked up at him.

"What…" she started to mumble. She looked around and everything was spinning slightly in rhythm with the pulsing in her leg.

"You fainted," Aiden explained as he helped her sit up.

"I sort of guessed that. I meant what was with the arrows?" she asked, rubbing her throbbing leg and wincing. Aiden handed her a piece of bread from the saddle bags. She ate it and took a drink of water. Her color had started to return after a few minutes.

"Let's get somewhere safe before I explain that. Are you up to riding?"

Ailia moved to stand and Aiden helped her up and held a hand out to steady her when she mounted Solas.

"Are you going to be okay up there?" Aiden asked as he mounted Iasair.

"Yeah, I'll be fine. How many more days must we travel until we reach the earth mage?"

"At this rate, we could get there as early as two days time."

"Oh. What about that…" Ailia hesitated slightly before finishing, "that whole arrow thing?"

"Let's get to camp and then I'll explain," Aiden repeated.

They spurred the horses on and traveled deeper into the forest until they came to the base of a tall mountain.

"Let's camp here for the night." He said. Ailia nodded and dismounted her horse trying not to put pressure on her leg. Aiden helped Ailia to sit and then brushed the horses but left the saddles on. Ailia directed Aiden to grab some pieces of cured meat from one of the packs. He handed a few of them to Ailia and he grabbed a few for himself. They both ate quickly. The air was humid and neither of them wanted to attract attention so neither moved to start a fire. Instead, they sat there and watched as the sun sank behind the mountain.

"This is the furthest I have ever been from Latzu," Ailia said quietly.

"How are you doing with that?"

"It comes and goes. So are you ever going to tell me what was going on back there." She answered.

"You're an Elementalist. What do you think happened?" He asked.

Ailia shook her head in disbelief, still refusing to believe what he was saying and what Kiana had told her. She asked him, "How can you be so sure?"

"Well, how much do you know about Magick?"

"What does that have to do with why you're sure,"

"Just answer the question," Aiden said.

"Not a lot really. I've only ever seen you be able to do any Magick. I could never talk about it or how it works for each person but when I was young Kiana explained how there are like two types of people but I can't remember what the difference between them is."

"Well that's true but let me expand on those two types of people. They are broad and loosely defined classifications. The first classification is by far the majority. They are those that can't use Magick at all. For almost all of this classification, they are fine to go about their daily lives without a thought towards the magic that they do not possess nor can never hope to. For the select few of this classification, they feel extremely slighted for their lack of ability. Drecan Undergallows happens to be one of these select few. That's only speculation though."

"Wait you mean to tell me that the only reason I was ordered dead is this? Over something I can't control or even knew I had." Ailia blurted out.

"Yes and the last classification is the one that you and I belong to. All people that have the innate ability to draw out the flow of Magick and make it do their bidding with little effort and sometimes without conscious knowledge. There is also a sub-classification that includes all the magical creatures like starlings, terrafirms, and the fairies. Most of the magical creatures of Mynor are in hiding right now because of the risks the Thren pose."

Ailia thought about all of this as she watched the sun move across the pale blue sky speckled with light wispy white clouds. Several birds flitted past and she watched them flit about for a while before looking at Aiden once more.

"What's it like being a mage?" She asked as she watched him twist a blade of grass between his fingers.

"Well at first it's weird like new things can be. Fire would follow me at first. I would walk past a torch and the flame would jump out to touch me."

"Did that ever go away?" she wondered out loud.

"With training, yes it did. For me, that was the first thing I worked on. I keep awareness around myself to let me know when a fire is near. Since I constantly look for it I don't get surprised. It allows me to safely walk past any flame without worry that it will jump to me. It also helps me remain undetected in unfamiliar places."

"Have you ever known an Elementalist, besides me that is?"

"Only in passing. You're the first I've actually known."

"Oh...,"

"Are you asking to figure out how your abilities will work?"

Ailia nodded and gently drew her knees up to her chest and pondered things for a short time.

"I used to think that my plants would look at me when I came near them and once I swear I saw vegetables growing before my eyes. I was probably just seeing things," She said softly and rested her chin on her knees.

"I believe you. Ailia you can control the four elements, why couldn't you control things like plants and how fast they grow," Aiden told her.

Ailia nodded but didn't seem to believe him. He chose not to press the issue knowing that she would come to believe in time as she rediscovered who she was. He pulled out the map to look at it.

"We should be able to reach Taryn in another two days' time with this pace." He said and then traced the path with his fingers so she could see.

"Okay, I'll take the first watch you should get some sleep."

Aiden put up little resistance to her idea. Using his pack as a pillow he quickly fell asleep. Ailia looked up at the sky and watched as the stars appeared one by one.

Ailia thought,

Ailia sat and took in her surroundings. Her eyes traced the craggy face of the mountain in front of them as well as the sparse line of trees they had emerged from. she felt the dirt beneath her hands and guessed this part of Mynor didn't get as much rain as Latzu.

Aiden slept for a few hours before he awoke to the song of a night bird. He looked at where Ailia had been sitting and found her dozing off. He watched as she fell into a deep slumber. The moon was still high in the sky so he let her sleep as he kept watch. When the sun rose she woke.

"Let me look at your leg," he said as he got up. Ailia untied the bandage as Aiden squatted beside her. He saw the shallow gash it was only partially scabbed with the cauterization he had applied earlier. Several spots had broken open with the movement from the saddle. The skin around it was a reddish pink.

"When you fainted earlier I burnt the wound shut but a few spots have broken open with the riding we have been doing," he told her as he touched it softly and she winced.

"If we were done traveling I would simply apply another layer of cauterization but seeing as we still have a while on the road I want to try something else. Are you okay with that?"

Ailia nodded and Aiden stood and went to his saddle bag. He opened up a pouch and grabbed several dried leaves. He rolled them and directed Ailia to hold them to her leg. He used a clean piece of cloth and wrapped the wound several times to secure the leaves in place and prevent dirt from touching the wound. Once the bandage was in place Ailia said, "Thank you."

"You're Welcome. That should help it heal a bit faster and relieve some of the pain you're feeling."

"Well, I guess you learned something from your medical training," Ailia chuckled softly and then braced herself and tried to stand. She was unable to muster the strength and looked up at him and asked, "Will you help me stand please?"

Aiden grabbed her hands and gently pulled her up. When she was standing she asked if he was ready to head out. He nodded and then helped her mount Solas before he mounted Iasair. They made their way along the base of the mountain until they reached a path. It was well hidden by underbrush and they nearly missed it but at the last moment Aiden spotted it and turned his horse towards it and Ailia followed.

The path was narrow and the footing sloppy so they took their time walking the horses much slower than either had anticipated. Each league they walked took them higher into the mountain range until they reached a fork in the path. To the right, the path sloped downward and to the left, it continued to climb. Aiden took out his map and then took the path to the right. As night fell they continued to trudge on by torchlight fueled by Aiden's fire. When the moon was high in the sky, Ailia noticed dark clouds started to roll in. The sky cracked loudly and a bolt of light hit the mountain. Rocks started to come crashing down.

"We have to keep moving," Aiden shouted over the commotion.

"We are going as fast as we can," Ailia shouted back.

The rocks kept falling faster as they continued to move forward. Ailia saw a rock coming towards Aiden with some speed and she shouted watch out. As she did her skin prickled again and the rock that would have knocked him off the mountain turned to dust and flew away with the wind. As the dust hit other falling rocks they too melted into dust and floated away. Aiden looked at her in amazement but didn't say anything until they were past the rock slide.

When the storm calmed he turned back to look at her and asked, "Was that intentional?"

"I'm not sure," she said, sounding exhausted.

They trudged on as the sky brightened from navy to lighter blue. As the sun rose stripes of pink and orange painted the sky. Aiden put out his torch and looked ahead of them, seeing the other side of the base of the mountain.

"We are almost through," he said and Ailia sighed in relief. By the time the sun had climbed fully into the sky they had made it through the mountains and they were both exhausted. They made camp at the base of the mountain. They hardly spoke as they grabbed some of the cured meat from one of the packs and ate quickly. Ailia jumped from the horse and barely winced as her feet hit the ground. Aiden let her take the first rest as the sun moved higher in the sky. At about mid day he woke her and then took his own reprieve. Ailia watched the sun move throughout the sky until they were once again covered by dusk.

Chapter Eighteen

When the stars began to twinkle that night they left the base of the mountain. Over the next day, they made their way over several large grassy hills and through some small patches of trees as they cut across the countryside of Mynor. Each time they stopped to rest Aiden took a look at her leg and was happy with the way the healing was progressing. by the time they reached the valley where Taryn lived what was once a gash was now a faint scab. On the sixth day since they had left Latzu they reached a small dry basin surrounded by several tall grassy mountains. Inside the basin was a small cabin.

Ailia took the lead while Aiden followed as they made their way up to the cabin. When they got closer, the door of the cabin opened. Out walked a tall woman wearing a tan skirt and a grass green bodice. Her fair blonde hair was braided in a detailed design.

"Who goes there?" She asked as Ailia hopped down from the saddle. Aiden also dismounted.

"My name is Ailia and this is Aiden."

"That tells me nothing," she said, taking a close look at the pair. She noticed that they were travel-worn and as she looked over Ailia, she noticed the green eyes. Not sure what to make of an

Elementalist showing up here, she asked, "Why have you come here?"

"We were sent here for several reasons but the main one is to ask you for your assistance."

"I am not in the habit of helping those I do not know."

"Do you know Kiana?" Ailia asked

The woman's eyes lit up in recognition of the name for a brief second and Ailia said, "She sent us here, to you, for help."

"That might be the case but what proof do you have of that?" she asked, still resisting the strangers.

Aiden opened one of his saddlebags and pulled out a talisman.

"This may ease your worries," he said and handed it to her. She looked over the talisman and then without words motioned them forward and closer to her home. She showed them where they could pen the horses. After the horses were safe the three of them walked into the house. As they walked in Taryn handed the talisman back to Aiden.

"Explain everything to me from the start," the woman said when they had sat down at the table.

"I am a captain in the Eolas. A year and a half ago I was sent to find the lost hope," Aiden gestured to Ailia and then continued, "I located her six months ago. Her kidnappers had raised her and I wanted to take my time getting to know her. Things changed drastically two weeks back when one of the kidnappers passed on. The thren didn't not give her a chance to declare her intentions and instead attacked. For her safety and the safety of the town a plan was hatched to get her the training she needed. Kiana, who was living in the same town as her, decided to keep her safe by sending us here. She hoped that we would be able to find refuge here with you at least for a time and that you would be able to train Ailia in Earth Magick."

The woman took a few minutes to think about what he said and finally replied, "My name is Taryn and I am an earth mage as you both already know it seems. I will not be easy but" she turned to Ailia, "I will be your first master. The road ahead of you will be long and difficult but worth the sacrifice. "

"Sacrifice I am familiar with and I will appreciate whatever you are able to teach me," Ailia said and bowed her head.

"There is no time like the present then. Shall we begin your training?"

Ailia nodded and Taryn led them through the house and out a back door. Behind her house, there was a large mostly hidden clearing that she would have sworn was part of the mountain. The three stood on the outside of the clearing for a moment or two.

"Let us start with the basics. I want to know where you are at. Summon me a rock," Taryn finally asked her.

"How? I know nothing about my powers. I've never used them on purpose before."

"That is unfortunate and this will make training a very long road for you then. Nevertheless, I made you a promise and I never back down from a promise. Are you really prepared for this?" Taryn questioned her.

"I am not sure but I have been told by more than one person I have no choice but to learn what I must."

"Aiden, why don't you go and unsaddle the horses. I am sure they are weary from the travels," Taryn suggested and he did so without question. Once he had left she turned back to Ailia and asked again, "Are you ready for this?"

Ailia took a deep breath and said, "I don't know. If it were not for a few emotional outbursts causing my powers to show I would doubt that I am an Elementalist. I don't know if I will ever be able to control anything but I want to try. If war is really coming to the whole of the land, I want to do my part to defend those who can not help themselves."

"You have a strong heart, Young one and that will serve you well on your journey. Do not forget your convictions."

Ailia nodded and then Taryn asked, "You said you had never used your powers on purpose but did you say that you have used your powers unintentionally?"

"Only twice that I know of once I stopped arrows that were flying at us and then I stopped a rock slide from hitting Aiden."

"Does it rain when you cry?"

Ailia nodded again and then Taryn asked, "Were your emotions overcharged when these outbursts happened.

Ailia just nodded not sure where Taryn was going with her questions.

Taryn continued to drill her about those instances by asking, "What were you feeling when the rocks almost hit Aiden."

Ailia looked to make sure Aiden hadn't returned before replying, "I didn't want him to get hurt."

"And the arrows?"

"After I got hit I could feel my skin start to prickle and I wanted to ask Aiden why that was happening but the arrows just kept coming and I just wanted them to stop and then they did."

"I am starting to see a pattern and while the whole picture isn't clear I do have an idea of where to start your training."

"When will that start?" Ailia took her turn to ask a question.

"We will start training you once you have recovered from your journey. You will need all the strength you can muster. How long ago was your leg hit?"

"We were attacked by rouges three days ago."

"Come into the house with me. I would like to take a look at it if you don't mind."

"I don't mind at all."

Ailia followed Tayrn into the house and was directed to sit at the table. Ailia did so and took off the bandage that had been tied to her leg for two days now. Taryn looked at the skin and found it to be almost completely healed. There were a few spots that still had a bit of a scab but the rest looked like the skin was well healed and that only a faint scar would remain as a reminder.

"Are you sure it was only three days."

Ailia nodded and Taryn kept talking, "This is incredible. You're almost fully healed. How did you accomplish that?"

Ailia shook her head and said, "I don't know, to be honest."

"That would be my fault. Before I joined the Eolas I was in training to be a healer," Aiden said as he walked in the front door from outside.

"That may come in handy and we shall have a discussion about what plants you used to achieve this at length. For today though you both need rest. I only have one extra room but you are welcome to it." Taryn pointed to a door before continuing, "You can bring in your saddlebags there should be enough room to store them in the room."

Aiden nodded and he went to carry their saddlebags inside. After they were settled inside he returned to the table.

"I will sleep out back under the stars. Ailia's rest is far more important than mine."

"Then it's settled, both of you get a good night sleep and training will commence tomorrow," Taryn said and headed to bed herself.

"Do you mind if I stay outside with you for a bit? I am not ready to sleep."

"Of course," Aiden said and he grabbed his pack and blanket from the bedroom before following Ailia outside. He found a spot of soft grass and the two of them sat together.

"How are you doing?" Aiden asked.

"I'm trying to take it day by day and not thinking about the bigger issues."

"That sounds like a good idea. I have every faith that you will be able to complete your training."

"I know," Ailia responded and looked up into the sky just as the first stars began to appear. When the moon was fully out Ailia excused herself and went back inside to sleep. Wondering what the next months would bring for her.

Made in the USA
Las Vegas, NV
24 September 2024

95733016R00132